I0457391

A LITTLE BIT NAUGHTY
A Moments in Maplesville Novella

Farrah Rochon

Nicobar Press

Special thanks to
A Glass Slipper by Duchess Productions
for providing the designer heel featured on this
cover.

A LITTLE BIT NAUGHTY
A Moments in Maplesville Novella

Chapter One

"What exactly is *this* supposed to do?"

Jada Dangerfield flipped over the box that held a red and black vibrator with three weirdly-spaced appendages. Her eyes and mouth both formed perfect O's as she studied the exceptionally descriptive pictures displaying exactly where the appendages were to be placed.

"Uh, okay. So this one may be a bit too advanced for me." She tossed the vibrator onto her coffee table with the others, and continued emptying the nondescript cardboard box that had been delivered a short time ago.

Bobbing her head to her Beyoncé Pandora station, Jada separated the bottles of flavored massage oils, warming lubricants and her current best-seller, the satisfaction enhancement gels, and checked each against the invoice that had been included with the shipment. Once everything was accounted for, she walked over to the tiny closet just inside the entrance to her equally tiny, one-bedroom apartment, and retrieved the hot pink polka dot rolling travel bag she used to cart around supplies for her Naughty Nights parties.

—

Recalling how skeptical she'd been when she first considered whether or not to embark on this venture, now all Jada could do was laugh at those previous doubts. She'd assumed the women of Maplesville were too prudish to attend a party that was essentially a thinly-disguised sales pitch for sex toys.

Wrong.

In the last six weeks, she'd learned that this sleepy little town was filled with ladies all too eager to get their freak on.

And thank goodness for that! The kinky little parties provided a welcomed boost to her income. In fact, her new gig as a Naughty Nights Consultant was the only thing keeping her head above water while she searched for a full-time job.

Jada stacked the packages of Ben Wa balls and bullet massagers — always top sellers — and zipped up the travel bag. She grabbed her cell phone from where she'd tossed it on the sofa, punching the speed dial for one of her two best friends, Kiera Coleman, as she rolled the bag to the door.

Kiera answered on the first ring. "I'm busy. What's up?"

"Well, hello to you, too," Jada returned, infusing much affront in her reply.

"Sorry. Hello," Kiera said with an apologetic sigh. "I'm busy. Can it wait?"

"I was just calling to let you know I got the

shipment for your party. I wanted to bring it over. You know I don't have much room here." Jada looked around her tiny apartment, which was a fraction of the six-thousand square foot home she once shared with her ex-husband, Eric. The bastard.

"Meet me at Mason's in an hour. I'm staying at his place tonight."

Jada scrunched up her nose. "Why?"

Kiera's older brother, Mason, was not her favorite person. She doubted Mason was even Mason's favorite person.

"Chinese drywall," Kiera answered. "I'll explain later. Look, I'm expecting a call—" As if on cue, a short beep came through the line. "I have to go, Jada. I'll see you in a bit." And then there was silence.

Jada stared at the phone for a minute, a bit mystified by the edginess she'd heard in Kiera's voice. She texted her, asking her to text Mason's new address again, then she went over to the folding card table she'd set up in a corner of her living room. It served as her dinner table, laundry-folding table, and computer desk.

She woke her laptop up from sleep-mode and logged into one of four job search engines she regularly used in her now eight-month search to find meaningful employment. The Naughty Nights parties provided much needed funds for her everyday living expenses, but it was not sustainable income.

—

There were several new job postings since she'd last looked earlier this morning. She emailed her résumé, tweaking her cover letter to fit the descriptions of each job. If she received even one call back from the ten résumés she'd submitted today, she'd count it a success. If that call back happened to be for the public relations position she'd applied for at a non-profit in downtown New Orleans, she would do cartwheels in the middle of the Maplesville Town Square.

Her phone chimed with an incoming text message from Kiera, who was apparently done with her all-important phone call. Jada plugged the address Kiera texted into the map app on her phone. Mason had recently built a house in a newer part of town that she'd never visited before.

She closed the window on the job search engine and checked the email account she'd set up specifically for her job search. After deleting the spam that had managed to circumvent her junk mail folder, she switched to her primary email account.

Her eyes landed on the first email and her stomach dropped.

"Shit!"

She forgot she'd set up an automatic renewal of her yearly American Marketing Association membership dues. Jada knew the small cushion she kept in her account wasn't enough to cover the two hundred-plus dollar renewal fee.

She pulled up her bank's online banking site and logged into her account. "Shit, shit, shit," she murmured as the site loaded.

"Oh, *shit!*" she said, dropping her head to her chin.

Just as she'd expected — and feared — the automatic renewal had caused her account to be overdrawn by eight measly dollars. She scrolled through the recent account activity and realized the check she'd written for her utility bill hadn't been deducted yet. If she didn't get money in the bank, she'd have *another* thirty-five dollar overdraft fee.

Jada put the laptop back into sleep-mode and went into her bedroom. She dragged the footstool from the foot of the bed to her closet and reached to the very back of the top shelf, feeling around for the old cardboard cigar box she'd gotten from her grandfather.

She lifted the flap and moved aside the old pictures and birthday cards, uncovering a simple white envelope. The money she kept in here was supposed to be for emergencies only. In the past eight months her definition of 'emergency' had been twisted and tweaked so much she wasn't sure what a non-financial emergency looked like anymore.

Jada grabbed a bottle of water from the fridge and carted her travel bag to her car. As she headed down Highway 421, the main

---

thoroughfare that sliced Maplesville into two halves, she noticed her gas needle getting cozy with the big E.

She groaned. It would have to wait. At the moment, making sure she didn't give the bank another thirty-five dollars she couldn't spare trumped filling her gas tank.

She pulled into the drive-thru lane at Maplesville Bank & Trust and cursed when she noticed the "Window Closed" sign. Maybe she should apply for a job at the bank. They could use the extra tellers.

She parked and headed for the double doors, slipping a twenty from the hundred dollars she'd taken from her emergency stash and shoving it in her jeans pocket so she could put gas later. She walked into the bank and stopped short at the sight of the huge, square-shaped head on the man speaking to the teller.

Eric Pearce. Hometown football hero. Most popular boy in school. Bastard of an ex-husband.

Seriously, the only way this day could get worse is if she were struck by a meteorite.

Actually, at the moment, a direct hit from a falling space rock would be preferable to facing Eric. He had the uncanny ability to make her feel as if she was the President and CEO of Loser Ex-Wives of America, due in no small part to the fact that while she had to scrounge for pennies just to cover her monthly bills, he was sitting on a mountain of family money that he'd astutely kept out of her reach in their divorce.

He was *such* a bastard.

Jada crossed her arms over her chest and jutted her chin forward as she stepped into the line for the sole teller. She did her best to avoid eye contact with Eric when he turned and started for the door, but, of course, he didn't take the hint.

He stopped a couple of feet from her. "Hi, Jada. You look…" His eyes trailed over her faded jeans and fitted Hello Kitty T-shirt. "Nice, I guess. How are things going?"

The false sincerity in his inquiry grated her nerves. Maplesville was a small town. He knew exactly how things were going for her, which is probably why he asked.

"Fabulously," Jada answered. "I'm trying out this new thing. It's called being happy. I had no idea such a thing existed."

"Maybe you should try this other new thing," he said. "It's called being an adult." He huffed out a grunt. "And you wonder why I left you."

Jada opened her mouth to tell him off, but nothing came out. She just stood there staring at him as he turned and walked out of the bank. His words stung more than she cared to admit.

Their relationship, which many had considered ideal — including her — had taken a sudden, toxic turn on their twelve-year anniversary, when Eric had asked for a divorce

———

after screwing her one last time. Bastard.

Her reaction had been somewhat lacking in the proper adult behavior department. When Jada discovered that he'd set things up to where she would get virtually nothing in the way of spousal support, she'd taken a swan dive right over the edge of sanity, reenacting every scorned woman scenario she'd ever heard of, including burning all of Eric's clothes on their front lawn.

It had not been one of her finer moments.

She was determined to shed the crazy ex-wife label. She would not allow a couple of admittedly gossip-worthy incidents to define her. And she refused to allow her ex-husband to continue fostering this fear that she would never be anything without him.

That's what she got for marrying at nineteen.

She went from being Montgomery Dangerfield's daughter straight to being Eric Pearce's wife. It was time for her to show the world just who she was. Though, she should probably hold off on that since, at present, she was an unemployed ex-public relations rep who sold sex toys to put food on the table.

She made her deposit which, thankfully, would cover the utility bill and leave her with a few dollars. She slid back behind the wheel of her Nissan Altima, the car she purchased used after selling the BMW she got in her divorce settlement, and pulled up the directions Kiera had texted. She checked the time on the dash, praying to God that Mason was still crawling his way through the notoriously thick evening rush hour traffic from downtown New Orleans to the north shore of Lake Pontchartrain. After her brief, yet dignity-destroying encounter with Eric, the last thing she needed was Mason Coleman looking down his nose at her.

Jada drove up to the gated entryway of Millwood Estates, one of at least a half-dozen subdivisions which had cropped up in this area that, not too long ago, was nothing but dense woods. She gave her name to the guard at the gate, who called Mason's home to confirm that she was indeed an invited guest.

"A bit pretentious for Maplesville." Jada snorted as she continued past the now open wrought-iron gate. Did they really have to announce guests in a town where practically everybody knew everybody?

She'd moved to Maplesville seventeen years ago, when the oil company her father worked for had relocated him to a refinery in South Louisiana. She'd seen more changes in the past two years than the combined fifteen years prior.

She wasn't a fan of the population growth spurt; it had added to traffic and was gradually stealing away the small town feel. But she couldn't begrudge the city dwellers who were ready for a taste of country living. Even though her parents had left Maplesville years ago when

---

her dad was relocated yet again, this time to Puget Sound, Jada had no desire to live anywhere else. This was home.

She wound her way through the subdivision, fighting the brief bout of envy that flashed as she drove past several displays of quaint family life: a father and son tossing a football in a front yard, an older couple cleaning out their flower beds together, several kids playing basketball in a driveway. Even the weather seemed to be in collaboration, the gorgeous spring day adding to the picture-perfect scene.

She wondered if it was a tenet of the Home Owners Association that every household look outrageously happy and content when unfamiliar cars drove through the neighborhood. As if she needed yet another reminder of what she no longer had.

Jada pulled up to a deep red, brick house with white shutters. It sat at an angle in a corner lot that butted against a wooded area at the very rear of the subdivision. This was her first time seeing the house Mason built last summer. Kiera had invited her to his housewarming, but Jada declined before her friend even got the words out.

Oil and water were bosom buddies compared to the way she and Mason got along.

Their mutual distaste for each other was no secret, though Jada had to admit to egging it on throughout the years. Going back to their high school days, she would say and do outrageous things just to get a rise out of him. It was her way of getting back at Mason for making her feel as if he was somehow better than her, which he'd managed to do from the very first day she met him.

Jada pulled into the driveway next to Kiera's compact SUV and tried to suppress yet another twinge of envy that shot through her as she stared at the house. She missed living in a nice, big, comfortable home. And Mason had this one all to himself. It was so unfair.

Of course, he probably couldn't pay a woman to live in this house with him. The man was the very definition of surly.

Taking out her phone, Jada called Kiera. "I'm here," she said, as she grabbed her travel case from the back seat and rolled it up to the front door.

The door opened and Kiera enveloped her in a hug. "I'm sorry," her friend said.

"For what?" Jada asked, returning the hug.

"For being bitchy on the phone. It's been a crazy day. The part for my mixer is stuck in a warehouse in Paducah, and I have to make six hundred puffed pastries on Saturday."

"Sounds like a problem."

"A huge problem," Kiera agreed, gesturing for her to come inside.

As she followed Kiera, Jada's lingering envy

---

brightened into a nice chartreuse color.

The house was gorgeous. It managed to be warm and inviting despite the museum quality décor. The living room and connected dining room were decorated in rich browns, tan, and a hint of blue, with large, masculine furniture and abstract paintings adorning the walls. It must have been done by a professional. She could not picture Mason taking the time to fuss over drapes and rugs and art work. Not Mr. Always Busy, High-Powered Attorney.

Jada suppressed a grunt. He'd had that self-important air about him way before he became an attorney. Back when they were in high school, Mason seemed more mature than some of their teachers. If one were to base their judgment solely on the way he acted, they would never guess he was only two years older than she and Kiera.

Jada could still remember that annoying way he would roll his eyes when they mentioned doing some of the normal things that normal teenagers did, as if it was a waste of time. Even though the family resemblance was unmistakable, Jada wasn't entirely convinced that Mason wasn't adopted. His stuffy demeanor was just too different from Kiera and her mother, who were both the biggest sweethearts on the planet.

"Why are you sleeping here again?" Jada asked. "You mentioned something about

Chinese drywall?"

Kiera's exceedingly irritated sigh spoke volumes. "It turns out the company that constructed my condo building may have used that drywall imported from China that was banned in the US for having harmful gases."

"Yikes."

"Tell me about it. The entire building has to be inspected. The management company is going to call sometime between tonight and tomorrow to let me know if my condo is affected." She put her hands up. "I so do not need this right now. I'm so mad I don't even want to *think* about this right now." Kiera nodded toward the travel case. "So, what kind of kinky toys are we peddling next week?"

Jada rolled the bag into the dining room and started pulling out the products she'd ordered for the party.

Kiera had the same reaction to the triple-threat vibrator that she'd had. "I'll have to graduate up to this one. I don't think I can handle that much stimulation," she said.

"I agree." Jada laughed. She took out fuzzy pink handcuffs, feather nipple clamps, and matching eye masks. "These were included in the Valentine's Day overstock sale, so I ordered a few just in case. Oh, and I still have to hit some of the drugstores for the Valentine's Day markdowns. I'm waiting for it to get to at least fifty-percent off."

"That sounds good," Kiera murmured as she absently rubbed the furry handcuffs, her unfocused gaze directed at a spot on the wall.

"Okay, that's enough of this." Jada slapped a rubber crop on the table. "What's up with you?"

Kiera looked over at her, blinking rapidly. "What?"

"I've known you too long. I know something is up."

"I've been put out of my house and may not have the part for my mixer. Isn't that enough?" she asked, tossing the handcuffs back into the travel case.

Jada slid her a skeptical look. She'd known Kiera since the day she and her best friend, Callie Webber, had caught Jada defacing the locker of the captain of the cheerleading squad. They'd taken her into their fold soon after and the three of them had been friends ever since.

Of the three of them, Kiera was the most optimistic. She rarely let anything get to her.

However, they all had their moments over the years, and Jada had known Kiera long enough to know that she wouldn't be able to pry anything out of her that Kiera didn't want her to know. She also knew that if she waited long enough, her friend would eventually open up.

***

Mason adjusted the intensity setting on the

driver's seat of his Mercedes CL550, groaning with pleasure as the rolling massage reached his lumbar region. He was actually happy to get stopped at the red traffic signal at the entrance of his subdivision. It gave him a few extra minutes to enjoy the seat's ministrations.

The light turned green and Mason turned into the subdivision, flashing his keycard up to the electronic keypad to open the gate. A few minutes later, he frowned as he pulled up to his house and spotted a white Nissan next to his sister's Mazda CX-5. It was blocking the entry to the side of the garage where he parked his car.

"Shit," Mason cursed under his breath.

He pulled in behind Kiera's SUV so that whoever was parked on the other side of the driveway could move out of his damn spot. Mason reached over to the passenger side and grabbed his briefcase and the mail he'd picked up from his post office box on the way home. He locked his car and walked up to the Nissan, peering inside. He noticed Hello Kitty seat covers and groaned.

"Oh, God, not her. Not today." Releasing a heavy sigh, Mason strode up to the front door and entered the house. "Shit," he said again when he confirmed that it was indeed Jada Dangerfield sitting in his living room.

"Nice to see you again, too, Mason," Jada said in a voice that belied her words.

"You're blocking the way into my garage,"

he said, pitching his keys into the top drawer of the apothecary chest that sat just off the right of the entryway.

Kiera rolled her eyes while Jada's narrowed with annoyance. Without another word Jada stood, pulled a set of car keys from the pocket of her tight jeans, and marched toward him, her gaze fiery enough to singe. Mason met her rage with a look of bored indifference, because he knew it would piss her off.

She stuck that pert nose in the air as she strode past him, leaving the door opened behind her. Seconds later, the rumble of a starting engine sounded from outside.

Mason advanced toward the sofa, thumbing through his mail.

"Why must you turn into an ass whenever you're around Jada?" his sister asked.

He looked up from the parcel of bills, credit card offers, and other junk mail. "Asking her to get out of my parking space makes me an ass?"

"Never mind." Kiera shook her head. "Anyway, thanks again for letting me stay here a couple of days. I could have gone to Mom's, but you're so much closer to my kitchen."

"I told you it's not a problem. It's not as if I don't have the room. Besides," he said, loosening the knot in his tie. "Having a caterer bunk here for a few nights means I don't have to worry about ordering takeout. The chicken pasta thing you make with the cream sauce will work."

Again with the eye roll, Kiera said, "The chicken is already defrosting. You're just that predictable."

Mason heard the front door open and grimaced. He'd meant to head to the back before Jada returned. He'd had a hard enough day at the office; he wasn't in the mood for engaging in combat in his own house.

"Happy?" she asked as she resumed her seat on the sofa.

"I don't know. Will I find a mysterious scratch on my door?"

"If I wanted to vandalize your property, I wouldn't do it behind your back, Mason. I'd make sure you had a front row seat."

"The way you did when you poured nail polish all over the hood of my Caprice?"

She hopped up from the sofa and got in his face. "I did *not* spill that nail polish on your stupid Chevy. How many times do I have to tell you that?"

"When I came home from tutoring, my car was fine. You walk through the door and, ten minutes later, the car is covered in bright pink nail polish. We don't need a CSI team to figure that one out."

"That ugly ass car needed a paint job, but I didn't give it one."

"Oh, my God, would you two please stop?" Kiera screeched. "What is it with the two of you?

You've been this way since high school."

"He's the one who starts with me," Jada accused, pointing her slim finger at his chest. Her own chest rose and fell with her labored breaths, pulling her fitted T-shirt taut across her breasts. As it had been way too often during their legendary arguments over the years, Mason had an overpowering urge to pull her against him and kiss the rest of the breath from her lungs.

Instead, as always, he took several steps back, giving himself some much-needed distance.

Kiera's cell phone rang, creating a fissure in the thick tension hovering over the room.

"Oh, it's my building's management office. Let's hope my place is okay." She answered the phone, but seconds later said, "Can you wait just a minute. The service here is spotty." Covering the mouthpiece, she hissed, "Why'd you have to build a house so far away from a dang cell phone tower?" as she headed for the front door.

Mason turned his attention from his sister's retreating back to find Jada giving him the evil eye again.

"What?" he asked.

"Forget it. Not worth it," she said before returning to her spot on the sofa.

Mason blew out a tired breath and headed for his room. He went straight to his walk-in closet, which was bigger than the combined bedroom and bathroom in the modest starter home he'd lived in for years before finally building this house.

He shrugged out of his suit jacket and hung it in the closet, then toed off his Tom Ford loafers, not bothering to put in the shoe trees. He'd probably wear them tomorrow.

There was a knock on the door to his master suite.

"Come in," Mason called. Kiera entered the room, and Mason could tell by her dour expression that she didn't come bearing good news. "Let me guess. Your entire condo was built using Chinese drywall."

"Every single inch," Kiera confirmed.

Mason shrugged. "It could be worse. You could also have termites."

"If you're trying to make me feel better, you're failing," his sister said. "Are you okay with me having an extended stay?"

"Yes, Kiera." It was his turn to roll his eyes. "Ask me again and I'm putting you out on your ass."

She laughed as she wrapped him up in a hug.

Mason would never admit it to her, but he'd pumped a triumphant fist in the air when Kiera had called this morning asking if she could stay at his place. It had been such a long time since she'd come right out and asked him for anything. He'd spent a fair portion of his adolescence and adulthood taking care of his sister; he missed her needing him.

"Oh, there's one other thing," Kiera said. "I was supposed to host a party at my place next weekend." She put both hands up, as if expecting him to protest. "It's nothing big. About ten or so women, and only for a few hours."

"Fine," Mason said.

"Great!" She gave him a peck on the cheek. "We were afraid we'd have to hold it at Jada's. Her place is so tiny you can hardly move around in there."

Mason almost added the caveat that Jada couldn't attend, but he didn't have the energy to be that petty. He just knew that he would have to stay the hell away if she was going to be there. Not that he had any desire to hang around with his baby sister and a group of her friends, but he sure as hell didn't want to hang around *that* particular friend. The woman got off on rubbing him the wrong way.

Kiera's cell phone rang again.

"Why are you so popular today?" Mason asked.

She looked at the screen and scrunched up her nose. "I need to take this." She gave him another peck on the cheek, and said, "Thanks again," before leaving the room.

Mason unbuttoned his cuffs and rolled the sleeves up on his shirt. After sliding his feet into his L.B. Evans slippers, he went to the kitchen and grabbed a bottle of water from the fridge, smiling at the chopped peppers, onions and other ingredients for Kiera's pasta, portioned in plastic baggies. Apparently, he *was* that predictable.

Sipping from his water bottle, Mason spotted the usually bare dining room table through the arched doorway that led from the kitchen. It was cluttered with boxes and packages. He went into the dining room and frowned as his eyes roamed over the collection of items strewn about the table.

He picked up a lavender box, his eyes widening in horrified surprise as he inspected the package.

"G-Swirl Vibrator?"

Mason marched into the living room and held the box up to Jada. "What in the hell is this?"

Jada looked up from the legal pad she was scribbling on — one of *his* legal pads — and peered at the box.

Like a saleswoman imparting the qualities of a new and improved product, she said, "This is the G-Swirl Vibrator, praised for its ability to elicit powerful orgasms quickly and effectively by stimulating a woman's G-Spot."

Mason choked back the instant rush of lust that lodged in his throat. Her matter-of-fact recitation had turned him on way more than it should have.

"I know what a vibrator is," he bit out. "What is it and the rest of that stuff doing on my dining room table?"

"It's for Kiera's party."

"What the hell kind of party is Kiera having?"

Releasing an exaggeratedly loud breath, Jada pushed herself up from the sofa and plucked the purple package from his fingers. "You may want to put this back," she said. "You break it, you buy it; and I doubt you're ready to handle something like this."

Mason followed her into the dining room where she set the vibrator on the table. Gliding her fingers along the collection of erotic toys, she picked up a box containing a silver egg-shaped device and held it out to him.

"You may want to start with this. It's popular with both males and females for stimulation of the erogenous zones. There is also an array of oils and gels designed to heighten sexual pleasure."

It took some effort for Mason to swallow as she went from one product to the next, her voice dropping to a sultry purr as she expounded on the benefits of each toy. Knowing Jada, the sole purpose of her little presentation was to make him uncomfortable. She'd succeeded, but Mason doubted she knew just what part of him in particular she was making uncomfortable.

"This, of course, is just an overview of what's available. If you're interested in products for a specific purpose, I'm sure we can find something that will work." She picked up a bright blue dildo and strolled over to him. With a decidedly wicked smile, she said, "Just so you'll know, personal demonstrations are extra."

Mason's entire being was immediately overwhelmed with a barrage of heat. He willed his body to fight the onslaught of arousal that rushed through him.

Folding his arms over his chest, he drilled her with a hostile look. "Why are you hell-bent on corrupting my baby sister?"

"Oh, for God's sake, Mason." Gone was the seductive lithe to her voice. It had been replaced with familiar ire. "You do realize your baby sister isn't a baby anymore, right? Brace yourself, but she isn't a virgin anymore either," Jada shared in a mock whisper.

He was in no mood to be mocked.

"What kind of party is this, Jada?" Mason asked in a voice that brooked no further bullshit.

She blew out another exasperated breath. "It's called a Naughty Nights party. It's not some orgy free-for-all, so lay off the crap about me corrupting Kiera. It's just a group of women having drinks and learning about sexual enhancement products."

"And you're the ring leader."

"I'm the sales consultant," she corrected.

"This may come as a shock to you, Mason, but some women actually like sex." She wielded the dildo. "Maybe you should join us for the party. I'm sure your puritanical ass can use all the help you can get when it comes to the bedroom."

Mason stared at her for several moments before reaching over and pulling the sex toy from her slim fingers. Flipping it around, he said, "It goes this way. If you're going to offer private demonstrations, you may want to learn how to use your products first."

He drained the remaining water from the bottle and left her standing in the middle of the dining room.

Chapter Two

Jada stood rooted to the spot where Mason had left her, shocked as hell.

And, okay, just a tad turned on.

Who would have thought that Mason Coleman, of all people, could make her cheeks heat with embarrassment, or make her nipples pebble as if they had been hit with a blast of freezing cold air?

Of course, it had been quite a while since her nipples had seen any action that wasn't of her own making, so it was understandable. But Mason? Mason Coleman? The one man she had never once thought of in a sexual way?

Actually, that wasn't entirely true. She could remember experiencing a twinge of interest once back when they were in high school. She'd gone over to Kiera's and encountered a shirtless Mason playing basketball with his friends in the driveway. But she'd only noticed him the way any hormonal teenage girl noticed a sweaty guy with nice abs and a decent face. And once he'd opened his mouth, any warm feelings she'd felt toward him had instantly chilled.

So why was her skin still tingling now?

Jada folded her arms across her chest, willing her nipples to calm down, and cursing Mason for putting her in this state in the first place.

Kiera came back into the house, pocketing her cell phone. Worry lines etched the corners of her mouth.

"Is everything okay?" Jada asked.

"Yeah," she said, waving off her concern. "Just work stuff. Nothing to worry about."

"I wouldn't say that. You've got at least one thing to worry about. Your brother was just in here. He isn't too keen on your kinky little party."

Kiera grimaced. "Ouch. Bet that was an awkward conversation."

If she only knew.

"Hey, can you spare an hour or so?" Kiera asked. "I was hoping you could come with me to my condo. I need to pick up a few more things since I'll be here for a while."

Jada shrugged. "I'm unemployed remember? I have all the time in the world."

"Thanks," Kiera said. She went to let Mason know she was leaving, then followed Jada out of the house. They walked over to Kiera's SUV.

"Oh, crap," she said. "I forgot I had all of this in here."

Jada peered into the smoke-colored windows, spotting boxes on the backseat and cargo area.

"I have to bring this stuff to my kitchen tomorrow," Kiera said.

"We can take my car."

"Are you sure?" Jada seared her with a look, and Kiera held both hands up. "Okay, okay. Thanks. Now I don't have to go inside and ask Mason to move his car."

Jada plunked a hand on her hip and pointed at the blue Mercedes. "What happened to him needing to get his car in the garage? I swear, your brother gets off on irritating me."

Jada wondered if she would later question why the thought of him getting off in any way whatsoever sent a zing through her bloodstream.

"I think you may be right." Kiera laughed as they walked over to the curb where Jada had moved her car. She shook her head as she opened the passenger-side door and slipped in. "What is it about you two? I have never seen two people who dislike each other so much? I know why Mason doesn't like you, but why don't you like him?"

Jada whipped her head around to her. "Why doesn't he like me?"

Kiera glanced over at her, her lips flattened in a frown. "He thinks you're shallow," she said. "But it's because he never took the time to get to know you," she quickly added. "And he and Eric were sworn enemies long before you ever moved here so I'm sure the fact that the two of you were a couple practically a week after you started at Maplesville High has something to do with it, too. And because you were a cheerleader. Mason always thought cheerleaders were superficial, but that goes back to the point of him believing you're shallow."

"Okay, I get it," Jada said, pulling away from the curb. After a few minutes, she said, "And to answer your question, I never liked him because he never liked me. And because he thinks he's better than everyone else."

"No, he doesn't." Kiera said, looking down at her phone, her thumbs flying furiously over the touchscreen. "Mason is very sweet. Except when he's around you," she tacked on.

Jada huffed out an aggravated snort as she flipped on her left turn signal to head south toward the commercial area where Kiera's condo was located. The building was yet another sign of Maplesville's rapidly expanding downtown area. It boasted a slew of new chain restaurants, retail stores, and a huge outlet mall that had beefed up the local economy. The downside was that it also made traffic an ever-loving nightmare on the weekends, when the town was inundated with visitors from all over the north shore of Lake Pontchartrain.

A flashing light on her dashboard drew Jada's attention. She thumped her fist against the steering wheel. "Dammit, I forgot about putting gas."

Jada glanced over at Kiera, whose face was intense as she read something on her phone.

"Hey," Jada called.

Kiera looked over at her. "What?"

"I just said that I forgot to put gas in my car and you didn't make a wiseass remark."

"Oh, sorry," she said, and went back to her phone.

Jada just shook her head as she turned into a filling station. Eventually, she would find out what had Kiera so distracted.

She pumped twenty dollars' worth of gas into her car and got back behind the wheel, waving off the bill Kiera tried to hand her as she reached for the hand sanitizer she kept in her glove compartment.

"Take the money, Jada. You're driving me to my place."

"I can afford to drive you ten miles to your house, Kiera. I don't need any more reminders that I'm a broke loser."

"I didn't say that!"

"You didn't have to. I had a reminder earlier today." She looked over at Kiera and let her head fall to the steering wheel. "I ran into Eric at the bank."

"The bastard," Kiera said. It was their universal name for her ex-husband. "What was he doing, taking a couple of hundred thousand out of that account he keeps in his sister's name so that you couldn't touch it in the divorce?"

"I didn't ask," Jada said. "I just got the hell out of there as soon as possible. It's a bit demoralizing to have to find spare change under my car seat just to pay my bills every month while he's sitting on a mountain of cash."

"I still would have gone after some of it in the divorce," Kiera griped. "This is a community property state."

"Which is why Eric Pearce is worth only about twenty grand on the books, despite the millions he has access to. He knew exactly what he was doing well before he filed for divorce."

"Bastard," Kiera reiterated.

Jada had to agree. It was amazing how quickly one could go from loving a person to wishing they would come in contact with a deadly, flesh-eating bacteria.

They made their way to Kiera's condo and were out of there in less than a half-hour. According to Kiera, the building's management company was footing the bill for movers to pack up and store all of the affected apartments' belongings while the walls were being replaced.

As they started back for Mason's, Jada considered just dropping Kiera off and leaving. After learning that Mason still thought of her as a ditzy, shallow cheerleader, she wasn't sure she would be able to stop herself from inflicting bodily harm when she next saw him.

However, an assault charge wouldn't help to dispel the crazy lady image she'd earned after the clothes-burning incident with Eric, so she'd resist the urge to knee Mason in the groin. Hopefully.

***

Mason rested his head against the firm leather headrest of the lounge chair in his office. Eyes closed, he allowed the soothing cadence of the jazz music flowing softly from the speakers mounted throughout the office to lull him into a state of relaxation he could only seem to find in this room. He brought the cut crystal tumbler to his lips, taking a sip of aged Dalmore Scotch. The expensive liquor felt like velvet against his tongue.

He rubbed the spot between his eyes, trying to blot out the bulk of his day.

The client whom he thought would be the ticket to an eventual partnership in the downtown New Orleans firm where he'd practiced tax law for the past eight years had turned out to be the biggest pain in his ass. But even without Oscar Davis's constant phone calls and emails, Mason figured he would still be nursing this headache. They were in the thick of tax season so, of course, every client had an emergency, and every single one of them thought their emergency should be his top priority.

And let's not forget his biggest headache of

the day, coming home to find Jada Dangerfield and her bevy of erotic toys.

Mason pitched the remaining alcohol down his throat, trying to wash away the memory of her seductive invitation to offer him a demonstration. He'd been semi-erect since the moment the words left her mouth, and had a feeling the only way he would get things under control down there was through some manual self-gratification.

Actually, he did have one tried and true method for quelling any amorous feelings.

Mason reached for his cell phone, and pulled his mother's number up on the speed dial.

"Hey there, Mason," she answered, and just like that, any lingering desire was instantly squelched by the sound of his mother's voice.

"Hey, Mom," he said. "I stopped by on the way home to check out your television, but you weren't there."

"I was at my Zumba class," she said. "And don't worry about the television. Linda Pennington's grandson came over and fixed it. Apparently, I had the input set to DVD instead of HDMI, whatever that means."

"Well, I can come over and we can figure out which inputs go with which settings," he said.

"It's already done. Joaquin even typed me up a little diagram. Oh, I'll have to call you later.

Linda's honking her car horn outside. We're going to check out the sales at the outlet mall."

"Okay," Mason said. "I'll talk to you later."

"Later, baby. Love you."

"Love you, too, Mom," he said before disconnecting the call. Mason set the phone on his desk and stared at it for several moments, trying to disregard the unease—possibly even resentment—stiffening his jaw.

He remembered a time when his mother wouldn't have even thought to get help from anyone else. Now, the last couple of times Mason had offered to take care of something around the house, he'd been usurped by some neighborhood kid who his mother had already called on.

He should be grateful. He had enough on his plate these days.

But taking care of his mother and Kiera had been ingrained in him. It had been his top priority since his fourteenth birthday, when he'd made a promise to his dad that he would always take care of them.

The week before, Mason had been hailed a hero for rescuing Kiera and his mother from their home after it caught fire from a faulty electrical outlet. His dad had been working the night shift at the local concrete plant. When he'd arrived at the burning house and learned from firefighters that Mason had gotten everyone out, he'd burst into tears. That night his father hugged him for a solid hour.

The next week, on his birthday, his father had taken him fishing—his favorite pastime back then. They'd had their first real man-to-man talk, and his dad made Mason promise that he would take care of his mother and sister if ever he wasn't there to do the job.

The following morning, at forty-two years old, he'd died unexpectedly of a massive heart attack.

Mason had taken the promise to heart, and spent his adolescence and adulthood caring for the two women in his life. He was having a hard time dealing with the fact that right now neither seemed to need him as much as they used to.

Mason pushed up from his chair and, despite his better judgment, returned to the dining room. He took a slow stroll around the cherry wood table, perusing the collection of toys, noting a few that he had first-hand knowledge of.

He felt sorry for those men who insisted they didn't need any extra help in the bedroom. He'd been introduced to the delights various enhancement products—as Jada had described them—could bring to the sexual experience by a woman he'd dated several years ago. He'd been the one to suggest their use in every relationship since.

The only problem was, it had been a while since he'd been in a relationship long enough to feel comfortable introducing any kind of erotic toys to the bedroom. The realization gave him pause. Maybe he needed to get himself a woman. It stood to reason that the stress he'd been under lately would be greatly reduced if he had an outlet for it.

Mason picked up a set of furry handcuffs and couldn't help but picture Jada standing there with that wickedly sexy smirk. The playful, hot pink fur looked like something she would choose. He closed his eyes as he trailed the soft fur between his fingers, and the previous situation in his pants roared to life yet again.

"Shit," he cursed with a sharp whisper.

His landline trilled and he tossed the handcuffs onto the table as if they'd bitten him. Mason stomped over to the kitchen and jerked the headset from the cradle with more force than necessary.

"Hello?" he answered.

"Hello, can I speak to Kiera Coleman, please?" asked the voice on the other end of the line.

Mason's forehead creased with his frown. Why was Kiera getting phone calls on his landline?

"Kiera stepped out for a minute," he said. "Can I take a message?"

"Would she be available on her cellular phone? She suggested I call this number first because the cellular service where she's staying

---

isn't ideal, but if she isn't there maybe her cell service is better wherever she is right now?"

"Who's calling?" Mason asked. "And what exactly do you want with Kiera?"

"I'm sorry, sir, but I'm not at liberty to discuss that. I will try Kiera at the other number she provided. Thank you," the woman said before hanging up.

Mason immediately searched through the Caller ID.

"Hammond Guaranty and Loan?"

Why in the heck would Kiera need to speak to someone at a loan office? She'd paid off the mortgages on both her condo and the building that housed her catering business; Mason had seen to it. And, to his knowledge, she still had a healthy sum left over from her portion of what had been paid to them through their father's life insurance policy. She shouldn't need a loan. And even if she did, why would she borrow from a finance company instead of coming to him?

Just as he was about to call her cell phone, he heard a car pulling into his driveway. Mason opened the front door and was met with a cardboard box, which Jada shoved into his hands.

"Here," she said.

He set the box on the floor next to the apothecary chest. "Where's Kiera?"

"Getting the rest of her stuff out of my car."

Mason moved past Jada and walked over to

the car. He lifted the armful of clothing from Kiera's arms and asked, "Why is there a loan office calling you?"

Kiera froze. "When did they call?"

"Just before you pulled up," he said. "Why do you—" Mason started, but Kiera was gone, turning and walking swiftly toward the curb, her cell phone to her ear.

Jada walked up alongside him and gestured with her chin. "Any idea what's going on with her?" she asked.

"You don't know?" Mason returned. He figured if anyone knew what Kiera was up to, it would be Jada or their other friend, Callie Webber. Those three were thicker than gravy.

She shook her head. "She's been acting weird all day. I figure she'll tell me when she's ready."

"I'm not waiting until she's ready," Mason said, tossing the clothes back into the open trunk.

Jada grabbed his forearm. "Just what do you think you're going to accomplish? God, Mason, you never change. When will you get it through that head of yours that Kiera is not some helpless child always in need of rescuing? Stop being a pain in her ass."

Mason's jaw clenched. He stepped up to her, and in a deceptively calm voice, said, "What goes on between my sister and me is not your concern. Stay out of it."

Jada folded her arms across her chest and jutted her chin in the air. "It is my concern when I have to hear about it from her. Kiera can take care of herself. She doesn't need you butting into her business."

He huffed out a laugh. "This probably won't come as a surprise to you, Jada, but you're the last person I'll take advice from regarding my sister."

Mason gathered the clothes from the Nissan's truck and started up the driveway. He was pretty sure he heard the word *asshole* muttered as he made his way back inside the house.

Chapter Three

Jada walked up to the glass doors of the beautifully landscaped club house on the grounds of Oak Grove Country Club in neighboring Covington, but she didn't open them. Not yet. She needed to collect herself; get her mind in interview mode. She adjusted her jacket, plucked a piece of lint from its collar, and pulled in a deep breath before grabbing hold of the door handle and pulling it open.

She was greeted by a receptionist with a friendly smile who instructed her to take a seat in one of the lobby's vacant chairs. As she made her way to her seat, she looked around the richly appointed room, taking in the marble columns, brilliant hardwood flooring and vases overfilling with fresh flower arrangements.

She wondered if the nauseous feeling bubbling inside her stemmed from the overall pretentiousness of the place or the fact that her ex-father-in-law was a member.

When she'd run across the job posting for the Membership Coordinator position, Jada had immediately disregarded it. Then she'd run across her utility bill and had returned to the posting. Not only did she meet every one of the qualifications, but the job would make use of her marketing degree and could possibly be a stepping stone to another position. Her mother always told her that beggars couldn't be choosers, and she was way past the point of begging. She was spiraling full-speed toward Grovel Ville.

The receptionist instructed her to go to the HR director's office. A half hour later, Jada drove out of the country club parking lot knowing that she wouldn't accept the position even if it was offered. The thought of spending eight hours a day feeding the egos of privileged businessmen and women by practically begging them to join a country club caused her to break out into hives. She'd risk high blood pressure from a ramen noodle-only diet before she reduced herself to working for this set.

She pulled into a drive-thru and ordered a burger and fries, something she normally wouldn't eat. But she'd skipped lunch and, dammit, she deserved to splurge every now and then. She figured if she was going to splurge she may as well go all out, so she added a milkshake to her order.

As she pulled onto I-12, heading east back toward Maplesville, she wondered yet again if it was time for her to call her parents.

"No," Jada said around a mouthful of truly

decadent French fries. She was not calling her parents.

Despite her rapidly dwindling savings, she was not ready to give up on herself just yet. Being a "surprise blessing" as her mother called her, she experienced more than just the normal baby-of-the-family treatment. Her sister, Angela, and brother, Montgomery, Jr., were sixteen and fourteen years her senior. Jada had been spoiled by both her parents and her siblings; never having to worry about anything because they were always there to catch her.

She'd immediately gone from the safety net her parents provided to being taken care of by her former husband. This was the first time she'd been required to stand on her own two feet. She would not cave, even if it meant peddling dildos and nipple clamps to every woman in the New Orleans metro area.

Jada exited the Interstate and pulled into the parking lot at the strip mall that had just been built on the very outskirts of Maplesville proper. She'd stopped in at the drugstore a couple of days ago and noticed that the Valentine's Day items had been marked down by thirty-percent. She figured they should be down to at least fifty-percent by now.

Jada grabbed a shopping cart and made a beeline for the aisle with the red clearance sale banner hanging over it. She grinned when she turned down the aisle and saw the "60% off"

———

stickers.

"Yes," Jada said with a fist pump.

She made her way down the aisle, throwing in heart-shaped garland, paper table centerpieces, and stuffed animals. They would make good door prizes.

Jada tried to stave off the sadness clawing at her chest as she pushed her cart past hearts with "Be Mine" written across them, and the boxes of chocolates. For twelve years Valentine's Day had been more than just a day for flowers and candy, it had also been her wedding anniversary. But a few weeks ago, her ex-husband, who had turned out to be the cruelest bastard to ever walk the planet, had turned her favorite holiday into a day she would forever abhor when he flew to Las Vegas and married his new bride on Valentine's Day.

It was the ultimate slap in the face. For the umpteenth time since he'd asked her for a divorce, Jada wondered how she could not have known that Eric could be so conniving, so *heartless*. He could not have simply changed overnight. It was as if she'd never really known him at all.

Jada shook off thoughts of Eric, which she had become adept at locking away in the back of her mind, and finished picking over the shelves. By the time she was done, her shopping cart was nearly full. She just hoped she sold enough products at her next couple of Naughty Nights parties to pay for this stuff before the credit card bill was due.

"Now I just need to find somewhere to put it all," Jada said as she stacked the bags in her trunk. God, she missed her big house with its ample closet space.

She suddenly realized that she wasn't too far from Mason's. Maybe Kiera could drive over so that she could unload it at his house.

Jada speed dialed Kiera. "Hey, I picked up a few decorations for your party. Do you have a minute to head over to Mason's so I can drop it there?"

"He's home," Kiera said.

"What?" Jada's head reared back. "On a Thursday afternoon? Isn't that against the workaholic's code of ethics or something?"

"I know, right? He took a vacation day. Said he needed to get away from the office for a bit. He said he would be home all day, but if you get there and he's not, just give me a call. It won't take me long to get there."

"Thanks," Jada said before disconnecting the call.

She wasn't sure if she wanted to go out to Mason's now that she knew he was there. She could only take him in small doses, and after their run-in a couple of days ago, she figured she'd met her quota of Mason Coleman for the month. Maybe even the year.

Jada drove up to the gate of his subdivision

and was surprised when she was waved in by the guard who was manning the gate the last time she was here.

"Seriously?" Jada snorted. What if she was a crazy ex-girlfriend who *wasn't* welcomed?

She'd suspected that the guard, like the gate itself, was just another way to provide a false sense of security for the former city dwellers who didn't realize they were moving into a town that saw crime about as much as it saw snow.

When she pulled up to Mason's, she spotted him on a ladder in front of the house, emptying debris from the gutters. Jada parked on the street, even though she could see his dark blue Benz was already parked in the garage.

She grabbed a couple of the bags of decorations from the back seat and started for the house, walking on the freshly cut grass.

She stopped a few yards from the ladder. "Hey, Mason, let me in the house. I need to put these inside."

He ignored her.

"Hellooo. Mason?" Jada called. That's when she noticed the thin wires coming from his pockets and going up to his ears. He dusted off his gloved hands and started down the ladder. When he was about four rungs from the bottom, he pulled the earphones from his ears and stuck them in his left pocket.

"Cleaning gutters?" Jada called. "That's what you do on your vacation day?"

"What the hell?" Mason turned around so swiftly that he lost his balance and went tumbling down the ladder.

"Mason!" Jada dropped the bags and rushed to him.

Well, hell. She didn't like the son of a bitch, but she didn't want to kill him!

***

"Holy shit," Mason muttered. He squeezed his eyes tight as he lay on his back, thankful that he'd gone with the Zoysia grass when his landscaper had given him various options. The soft, dense ground cover had probably saved him from a broken hip.

"Mason, wake up! Oh my, God, do you need to go to the hospital? I should call an ambulance."

"Shit," he whispered again. Jada's frantic nattering wasn't doing a damn thing to help the headache that had instantly sprouted up behind his eyes. He lifted one eyelid and noticed her dialing on her cellphone. "No," Mason said.

"Hello, I need to report an emergency," she spoke into the phone.

"No!" Mason said with more force. He flinched, his headache mushrooming.

Jada pulled the phone from her mouth. "Are you sure?"

He attempted to nod. "Yes. I'm fine."

"You're not fine."

"I don't need to go to the hospital," he said.

Mason tried to brace himself up on his elbows, but the sting that shot up his right arm had him grimacing and falling back onto the grass, the blades tickling him through his threadbare T-shirt.

He heard Jada apologize to the 911 operator. Seconds later, she was on her knees next to him, running her hand over his head.

"Do you think anything is broken?" She ran her palms over his shoulders and down his arms, her soft skin leaving a tingly sensation along his nerve-endings.

He did *not* need this. If she didn't stop touching him, his baggy, nylon basketball shorts soon wouldn't be able to camouflage the likely consequence of having her hands all over him.

"I'm so sorry, Mason. I swear I didn't mean for you to get hurt. I am so, *so* sorry."

Mason cocked one eye open and peered up at her. "Am I really awake, or did I bump my head and knock myself unconscious?"

"Of course you're awake," she said. "Why would you ask that? Do you think you have a head injury or something?"

"I asked because you're being nice to me."

She rolled her eyes, and Mason felt a slight grin creeping up the corner of his mouth.

"Come on," Jada said, hooking her arm around his uninjured elbow and lifting him up.

"Let's get you in the house and get these scrapes cleaned up."

His first instinct was to tell her he could handle cleaning up the cuts on his own, but just these few minutes of her fussing over him had felt so good, he decided to keep his mouth shut. Mason allowed her to help him into the house, using the opportunity to inhale her light, clean scent. She smelled fresh, like cotton or baby powder or one of those other soft feminine smells. It was a lot better than he smelled after an afternoon of cleaning out gutters and doing yard work.

They went into his kitchen and Jada pulled out a chair at the small, round table in the breakfast nook.

She pointed at the chair. "Take a seat."

Damn if she wasn't bossy as hell.

Damn if he didn't love that about her.

Mason sat and pinched the bridge of his nose, blowing out a frustrated breath. The irony of his long-standing attraction to this woman was both tragic and amusing. She was the *last* person he wanted to be attracted to, yet he'd been done for from the very first moment he'd spotted her walking into the library at Maplesville High.

She hadn't noticed him, of course. Even though he was an upperclassmen, he'd been so far out of Jada's league that he hadn't rated a passing glance. Mason had often wondered over the years if she would have *ever* noticed him if not for her friendship with Kiera.

The only thing that surpassed his attraction to her was the utter resentment he harbored toward her for never seeing him as anything other than Kiera's older brother. He resented her for feeding into the stereotypes he abhorred; the popular cheerleader marrying the dumb, rich jock. Most of all, he resented the fact that when he was around her she made him feel like that introverted kid who couldn't possibly catch the eye of a girl like her.

But he wasn't that kid anymore. And over the years he'd managed to catch more than just the eye of women who were just as beautiful as Jada. Maybe now that she'd finally seen Eric for the asshole he had been since birth, she could open her eyes to the possibility of being with someone like him.

Being with someone like him?

Mason ran his hands down his face.

What in the hell was the matter with him? He'd gotten over his infatuation with her a long time ago. He did *not* want Jada Dangerfield.

"Are you sure you don't need to see a doctor?" she asked.

It was one thing not to have her barking at him, but to hear actual concern in her voice? That had to be the reason all these old feelings were resurfacing.

"I told you I'm fine," Mason said.

She grabbed the dishtowel he'd left on the counter and folded it. Then she gently lifted his arm, slid the towel underneath, and placed his arm on it. Mason couldn't tear his eyes away from her delicate fingers as she handled him with such care.

She shrugged out of the jacket of the charcoal gray suit she wore and hung it on the back of a chair. Then she put her hands on her hips. "You're Mr. Responsible, so I know you have a first aid kit somewhere."

Resigning himself to the fact that she seemed determined to help him, he nodded toward the walk-in pantry. "Second shelf from the top."

She turned toward the pantry and his eyes went straight for her ass. The slim skirt hit just below her knees. The conservative length didn't show off her legs as much as he would have liked, but the way the material hugged her backside more than made up for it.

Her body had held a prominent place in his fantasies back when they were in high school, especially during football season, when she ran around town in that sexy cheerleader uniform. It used to hug her petite frame perfectly, flowing just right over her curves.

He'd come home one weekend, back when he was an undergrad, to find that the squad had switched to uniforms that bared her midriff. Mason had made the trip home every Friday after that, and not because he gave a damn about

—

the football team.

As she stood up on her toes searching for the first aid kit, the skirt rode up ever so slightly, and the appendage in his lap twitched to life.

"Oh, you are so busted, Mason Coleman."

Mason's eyes flew to his lap. He looked back up at her just as she turned, holding a pack of Little Debbie brownies.

"You've got jars of protein powder, flax seeds, and all that other healthy crap, but it's all just a front, isn't it?"

"What can I say?" Mason said with a shrug. "I've got a weakness for Little Debbie. She knows exactly what it takes to please a man."

Jada's laughter echoed around the kitchen. She brought the box of brownies, along with the first aid kit, back to the table. "If you don't whine like a baby while I clean those scrapes, you can have a brownie as a reward."

His brows lifted.

"I'm not completely evil," she said.

"I never said you were," Mason replied.

One corner of her mouth lifted in a grin as she took the seat at a right angle to his. Her normally wavy hair was straight, and falling just past her shoulders. It matched the severe look of the suit.

"Let's take a look at this," she said, reaching for his arm. She inspected the scrape, which still stung to high heaven. "It doesn't look too bad. I've seen worse."

"Really? Where?"

Jada popped open the latch on the first aid kit and took out several packets of wrapped gauze, alcohol wipes, and antibiotic ointment. "Don't tell anyone this," she said. "But I'm just a tad bit of a klutz."

"Nah, you?" Mason said in feigned surprise. "I had to patch up the hole you made in Kiera's bedroom wall when you all were trying to learn the dance from that stupid movie, remember?"

Her brilliant brown eyes lit up with laughter. "Oh my, God. I'd forgotten all about that."

"Ouch," Mason hissed as she dabbed the cut with an alcohol wipe.

"Sorry," Jada said. She leaned forward and gently blew his roughed up skin, and the arousal he'd been trying to stave off came roaring back to life. "Better?" she asked.

He nodded, and after swallowing past the knot of lust wedged in his throat, said, "Much."

Neither of them moved as their eyes locked, time suspending for just a moment. There was a charge in the air that traveled along his skin, making it pebble with goose bumps despite the heat coursing through his bloodstream.

Jada was the first to look away, shaking her head and expelling a breathy laugh.

"You know, my klutziness went far beyond getting my foot stuck in Kiera's wall," she said. "I'm surprised I didn't land in the hospital.

—

Although, I did come close." She looked up at him, her latte-colored cheeks turning a shade of pink. "At the homecoming game my junior year, I broke my wrist doing a cartwheel, but I didn't tell anyone because I didn't want to miss the end of the game."

He couldn't avoid the cynical hitch of his brows.

"Hey, homecoming was important," she defended. "The team needed us."

"I didn't say anything," Mason said.

"You were about to."

Yes, he was. His aversion to the girl she'd been back then, and all she'd represented, was so strong it was still hard to shake it, even after all these years. It was unfair to hold it against her. Being one of the most beautiful, popular girls in school wasn't a crime.

"I was going to say that you were pretty brave," Mason said instead. "The Maplesville Mustangs were lucky to have you cheering them on."

Her look was guarded, but she only said, "Thank you," before returning her attention to his arm. She cleaned out the bits of dirt and grass and applied a generous amount of antibiotic ointment before covering it with a piece of gauze and applying white tape to all four sides.

"All done," she said, giving the bandage one final pat. She started to pull her hand away, but

Mason stopped her, capturing her wrist with his other hand.

Jada looked up at him, her eyes filled with…what? Curiosity? Interest? He wasn't sure yet, all he knew was that it didn't hold the disdain he usually got from her.

"Thank you," Mason said, his voice suddenly hoarse with the want gripping him.

"It was the least I could do," she replied with an equally husky quality to her voice. She cleared her throat. "After all, I'm the one who caused you to fall."

Mason shook his head as he leaned in a touch closer. "It was an accident."

Jada's eyes dropped to his lips. Her chest rose and fell with each breath she took as she stared at him. Mason edged forward, closing the space between them.

The shrill of her cell phone broke the silence.

They both jumped. Jada hopped up from the chair, fumbling the phone as she tried to answer it.

"Hello?" she answered. "Hello? Kiera?"

Mason slouched back in his chair. "The service isn't good in here," he muttered, running his hand down his face.

Jada held the phone to one ear and covered the other with her free hand.

"Yes, I got in," she said. She glanced at him. "Mason was here. Look, Kiera, I'll call you in a minute, once I'm in a better service area." A pause, then, "Okay, bye."

She ended the call and looked over at him. "That was Kiera," she said unnecessarily. She pulled in a deep breath. "I should get going."

Mason nodded. The wad of pent-up lust clogging his windpipe just dared him to try to get a word out.

"Okay, uh. Bye," Jada said with a jerky wave. She rushed out of the kitchen like the house was on fire.

Rubbing the back of his neck, Mason ambled over to the front door so he could lock it behind her.

Just as he approached, it swung open again, and Jada came inside, carrying two plastic shopping bags. "I forgot these outside. They're decorations for Kiera's party."

She set the bags on the floor and did an about-face. She closed the door behind her, then a second later, came back inside.

"I forgot my jacket," she said, marching past him into the kitchen, returning with her suit jacket. "Tell Kiera I'll talk to her later." She shook her head. "What am I saying? I can call her myself."

The nervous laugh that fluttered from her was as telling as anything else. When had he ever seen Jada flustered? The fact that *he* was the one who'd put her in this state caused a ripple of satisfaction to course down his spine.

She turned with her hand on the door

handle. "Try not to get that bandage wet."

Mason nodded. "Thanks again for tending to me."

"You're welcome," she said. Then, with an overly-bright smile, she walked out.

Mason stood just inside the doorway, watching as she got in her car and drove away. He knew he would spend the rest of the afternoon trying to figure out just what in the hell had happened these past twenty minutes. He wouldn't be surprised if he woke up to discover that he really had bumped his head, and the moment that passed between them at his kitchen table had been nothing but a dream.

Because only in his wildest dreams had he ever been so close to laying his lips on Jada Dangerfield's.

Chapter Four

"Now, ladies, if you want to take naughty to a new level, you may want to consider the 'Spank Me' package." Jada held up the black satin sashes and blindfold, along with the rubber-tipped crop.

"I don't know. I bruise easily," one of the women said. "Now, if I can use this on my husband we just might have a deal."

Jada sliced through the air with the crop a few times. "The 'Spank Me' package knows no gender," she said, setting off a round of whoops, hollers and catcalls.

She set the crop on the table and picked up the straps of the swing. "If you're feeling *really* adventurous, the Naughty Swing will definitely put some spice back into your life."

"What in the world do you do with that?" another of the guests asked.

"It hangs from the doorframe and makes it possible to get into a number of positions," Jada answered.

The woman who had introduced herself as the hostess's sister raised her hand. "I can attest to this one. I have it and it does wonders."

"Oh shut up, Valencia," another said. "You have just about everything she's pointed out. I always knew you were a freak."

"Don't hate," Valencia said before wrapping her lips around a penis-shaped straw and sipping her mojito.

"What about this?" Another woman asked, holding up the canister of warming gel.

"This is one of our many sexual enhancement gels," Jada answered. She went into her practiced spiel, describing what each gel provided, and answering questions about their safety.

"Okay, ladies." She clapped her hands together. "Take a few minutes to look these over, and then we'll get to the fun stuff…the kind that vibrate."

Another round of catcalls resounded around the room.

As the women perused the products, Jada walked over to the refreshment table at the far end of the large den.

Monique Walker, her hostess for tonight's party, walked up to her. "This is so much fun, Jada. Thanks for coming all the way out here."

"It was no problem at all." Based on the number of orders she'd taken already, the commission she would make on tonight's Naughty Nights party would more than cover the expense of traveling nearly an hour from Maplesville. "It looks as if the ladies are having a good time," she added.

"I knew they would." Monique grinned. She leaned in closer and whispered, "You know, I wasn't sure about that swing when you showed it to us at Joelle's bachelorette party, but after hearing Valencia, I may just have to give it a shot. I'll just make sure to put 911 on speed dial," Monique said with a laugh.

Her mention of 911 instantly conjured up the call Jada had made yesterday, and a shudder of need swept through her. It had become a common occurrence whenever her mind even tiptoed in the vicinity of thoughts about Mason and their sexually-charged exchange.

She had pretty much convinced herself that their near-kiss had been the result of Mason bumping his head and experiencing a slight touch of concussion-induced insanity. She still hadn't figured out exactly why she had been ready to return his kiss. If Kiera's call hadn't interrupted them, she would be standing here right now with intimate knowledge of the way Mason Coleman tasted.

Another shudder shimmied down her spine.

"Get a grip," Jada mumbled. She swiped a couple of carrot sticks from the vegetable tray before rejoining the party. She wandered over to a glass-topped sofa table where several women were looking over the flavored oral gels, massage oils, and edible body paint. Jada explained how to use the items and deftly dodged questions about which one her man preferred. The hardest part about this job was trying to sell items to women who expected her to have full knowledge of how everything worked. It was embarrassing to admit that she didn't have anyone to try them out with.

She shut down the mental image of Mason before it could firmly take root. She would *not* go there.

Jada clapped her hands to get the room's attention. "Are we ready to play the 'Can You Guess the Lube Flavor' game?"

The doorbell rang and Monique waved at her to continue as she stood to answer the door. But before Jada could continue with the party game there was a loud squeal at the door.

Monique interrupted, calling, "Ladies, ladies! The newlywed is here. Jada, you should make a *lot* of money off of her."

Jada looked up to find the new Mrs. Eric Pearce walking through the front door.

Rage, raw and primitive in its intensity, gripped her. She managed to quickly rein it in, counting it as a small victory that she didn't immediately go all *Real Housewives of Atlanta* on Nikki Pearce. At least she was starting to show some growth from the woman who burned her ex-husband's clothes on the front lawn.

Monique and Nikki joined the rest of them in the den and Jada took a measure of satisfaction in seeing how uncomfortable her ex-husband's new wife seemed.

Willing her voice to remain cool, Jada said, "Hello Nikki."

"Uh, hi Jada," she answered.

"Oh, you know Nikki?" Monique asked.

With a smile that she knew had no choice but to look fake, Jada said, "Why don't we get this out in the open?" She gestured to the other woman. "Nikki's new husband is my ex-husband."

The awkward silence that came over the room was akin to a funeral more than a fun Girl's Night Out party.

Jada put her hands up. "It's not a problem for me. Is it one for you, Nikki?"

She shook her head. "No. No it isn't."

The girl could not be more than twenty-years-old. Eric really should be taken out to a field and shot like a rabid dog.

"Okay, then. Let's get back to the naughty stuff," Jada said, still wearing that fake smile that was starting to make her jaws hurt. Continuing with this Naughty Nights party ranked up there with wearing underwear made out of poison ivy leaves on the list of things she most wanted to do, but Jada soldiered on.

She deserved a Golden Globe, or better yet, to be canonized into Sainthood, for the way she was able to maintain her affable facade as she suffered through the women joking about Nikki using the different sex toys with her new husband. Jada laughed and snickered with the rest of them as she mentally counted down the minutes until she could wrap this party up.

She was so close, so very, very close to making it through the night with her emotional well-being intact…until Nikki dropped a bomb that imploded her world.

Holding up the Naughty Swing by its leather-covered swing chains, Jada asked who would be brave enough to buy it.

With a cagey smile, Nikki rubbed her belly and said, "I don't think that's safe for a pregnant woman."

All of the women squealed, showering Nikki with hugs and well-wishes.

Jada attempted to offer congratulations, but her ability to consume bad shit and grin only went so far. This was the kind of blow that took everything out of her.

She turned to Monique. "Can you take the last few orders for me? I need to run to the restroom."

On shaky legs, she made her way to the hall bathroom. The minute she closed the door, silent sobs poured out of her. She covered her face with her hands and slid down the door, crumbling in a heap on the floor.

She could deal with everything else — the raunchy jokes about Nikki and Eric using the sex toys, the infuriating knowledge that her ex-husband was apparently much more attentive in

---

bed with his new wife than he had ever been with her — but not this. News that Eric would be a father, after all the years of her trying and never being able to carry a pregnancy to term, was too much for her emotionally-drained mind to withstand.

Jada hugged her arms around her waist, unable to stop the pain radiating from her womb.

It was just so incredibly unfair. Hadn't she been through enough this past year? The total annihilation of her marriage, losing her job, having to give up her home and the life she knew. And now this?

How many times had she dreamed of lying in a hospital bed cradling Eric's child in her arms while he stood at her side, the proud, boasting new father? She'd come close twice, but her dream never made it past the first trimester. Now Eric would get his baby, and she would be left with nothing. It had become a sad, reoccurring commentary over the past year.

Jada forced herself to stand. She splashed water on her face, patting it dry with a hand towel. She stared at herself in the mirror for several more moments. She wanted to make sure there were no lingering signs of her mental breakdown.

When she returned to the den, many of the party attendees were packing up and preparing to leave.

Monique walked up to her, order forms in hand. "I have some orders, but others took down the website so they can go over the products with their husbands. I passed out the business cards with your consultant number to be sure you get the commission."

"Thanks," Jada said. "And thanks again for hosting a party. If you know of any other friends or colleagues who may want to host one, give them my card. I'm more than willing to travel outside of Maplesville."

"I will," Monique said. She bit her bottom lip, and in a lowered voice, said, "And I'm sorry about Nikki. I swear I had no idea."

Jada waved off her concern. "Don't worry about it. Really, it's fine."

"You're more understanding than I would be," Monique said. "My sister said the rumor around the office is that Nikki was dating her husband before he was even divorced."

"The rumor would be true," Jada said. "Which makes me the luckiest one of the three, don't you think?" She smiled and went over to pack up her travel bag.

By the time she rolled the suitcase out to her car and loaded it in the trunk, Jada felt as if she would crack into a million pieces with just the slightest touch. Tonight had just been *too much*!

She waved goodbye to Monique and backed out of the driveway. The tears started flowing down her cheeks before she reached the stop sign at the head of the street, and by the time she drove onto the highway the torrent was coming so fiercely that she had to drive one-handed, the other too busy wiping away tears.

She cried until her chest hurt. She cried like she had not cried in over a year, since the night Eric had given her an ultimatum after they'd made love: either allow him to see the woman he had been sleeping with behind her back, or give him a divorce. She cried as much as she'd cried both times she'd received the crushing news from the ultrasound technician, telling her there was no heartbeat.

Gripping the steering wheel with both hands, she cried until her throat was raw with it. She'd remained strong as long as she could; she was due this cry.

Her car jerked and sputtered, then started to lose acceleration.

"What the…" Jada wiped her face and looked at the dash. "Oh, God. No," she moaned.

The car jerked again.

"Dammit!" She banged her fist on the steering wheel before guiding the car to the shoulder of the highway.

She was out of gas.

She folded her hands on the crest of the steering wheel and dropped her head on it. How else had she expected tonight to end?

Maybe if she hadn't been crying her eyes out, she would have remembered to put gas at the filling station she'd spotted on her way to Monique Walker's house.

"Dammit!" Jada said again.

She pulled up the number for AAA in her phone and dialed. She quickly hung up, remembering that she had not renewed her membership, considering it a luxury she could no longer afford. Funny how quickly a luxury turned into a necessity.

She pitched her head back against the headrest, trying to decide which of her friends would be able to refrain from shouting *"I told you so"* in her ear. Probably Callie.

Of course, calling Callie had its disadvantages. Ever since she'd started dating her new boyfriend, Stefan, she was nothing but sunshine and roses. It was sometimes hard for Jada to rein in her envy, which made her feel like a total bitch for begrudging her friend's happiness.

Just as she was about to call Kiera, a car pulled up behind her.

"Oh, shit," she murmured. She hit the automatic door locks and positioned her fingers over the keypad so that she could dial 911 if necessary. She kept her eyes on her rearview mirror, her heart pounding as the driver's side door opened. The interior of the dark car lit up and Jada let out another groan.

"Seriously? Of all people?"

Her heart continued the rapid hammering as

Mason walked up alongside her car. She pressed the down button, bracing herself for his censure as the window descended.

"Car trouble?" he asked.

"Do you stop for all stalled vehicles on the side of the road?" she asked. "How did you know I wasn't some crazy serial killer who pretends to have car trouble to lure his victims?"

"I considered that for a moment, but I figured serial killers don't have shiny, metallic Hello Kitty bumper stickers that you can see from a mile away even in the dark."

"Good point," she drawled. "And it's not car trouble; I ran out of gas. *Please*, don't tell your sister. I'll never hear the end of it."

"You do realize that's one of the easier car problems to prevent, right?"

Jada rubbed her eyes with the heels of her hands. "Please, Mason. Tonight is not the night for a lecture." She dropped her hands and sighed. "Not tonight."

Mason reached inside and unlocked her car door. "Come on. I'll drive you to a filling station and get a portable gas can. That'll get you enough gas to get back to the filling station so that you can fill your tank."

He opened her car door and the cabin was awash in light.

"Jada, what's wrong?" Mason fell to his hunches and captured her chin in his fingers. "You've been crying."

She ducked her head and wiped at her cheeks. "It's nothing. I'm fine."

"If that was the case you wouldn't have tracks down your cheeks."

"I'm fine, Mason. Really," she insisted, but her shaky voice betrayed her. Jada bit her trembling bottom lip, but she no longer possessed the strength to hold it all in. The dam broke again.

She dropped her chin to her chest and allowed the tears to fall with singular abandon.

She felt Mason reach over her and feel around for the keys. He took them out of the ignition, then he wrapped an arm around her back.

"Come on," he said. "I'll bring you home."

"No." Jada shook her head as she got out of the car. "Just take me to the filling station."

"I'm not letting you drive home in this condition."

"It's not as if I'm drunk, Mason."

"Crying your eyes out while you're trying to drive is just as bad. Your car will be fine until tomorrow morning. Come on."

Jada hesitated for only a moment before reaching in to grab her purse from the floorboard on the passenger side.

As they walked to his car, her footsteps halted.

"One second," she said as she used her key fob to open the trunk.

She'd paid too much money for the consultant package to chance someone breaking into her car and stealing it. She reached in for the travel case, but Mason stepped around her and grabbed it. His other hand went to the small of her back as he escorted her to his car and held the passenger door open for her. Once she'd slipped by him, he closed the door and deposited the travel case on the backseat.

Jada just stared at him as he walked around the front of the car to the driver's side. His navy blue suit must have been tailored because nothing off the rack could fit so perfectly.

He got behind the wheel, but left the door slightly ajar, preventing the overhead light from shutting off. Jada was tempted to reach above her head and turn it off manually. She could only imagine how blotchy and puffed up her eyes must look after the crying fest she'd been engaged in for the past forty minutes.

"You know what kills me?" Mason asked. "The fact that you use such an innocent-looking bag to carry around all of those kinky toys." He looked over at her and his face broke out in a smile. That's when she realized he'd been teasing—not judging—her. Mason Coleman was actually trying to make her feel better.

Jada returned his grin. "What do you suggest I use? Something made out of red and black lace?"

He shook his head. "Nah, stick with the

polka dots. The shock factor you'll get when you open it up and start pulling out all those toys is that much better." He looked over, his eyes glittering with mischief. "I know it shocked the hell out of me."

Jada choked out a laugh as Mason closed the door, started the car, and pulled out onto the roadway.

***

As his tires ate up the miles of the highway, all Mason could think about was Jada being stranded on the side of the road if it were not for him leaving the office much later than usual tonight. She probably wouldn't have been stranded for long — she'd told him that she was just about to call Kiera when he'd pulled up behind her — but the fact that she'd been on the highway alone, in the dark, sent a tremor of unease down his spine.

She sat with her chin in her hand, looking out the passenger-side window. Mason debated whether or not to engage her in small talk. He wasn't sure engaging Jada in any way was good for his peace of mind.

Confusion over the moment that had passed between them when she'd cleaned the cut on his arm had plagued him since yesterday. He had resigned himself years ago to the fact that his long-held attraction to her just wasn't going away. He'd decided to view it as a nuisance; something that was easy to ignore because of the toxicity of their relationship.

But something had changed yesterday. The biting sarcasm and cynical quips that had always been the hallmark of their interactions had taken a backseat to Jada's thoughtful, tender consideration for his well-being. Having her treat him with something other than scorn enticed those barely submerged feelings of attraction, beckoning them to the surface.

But the fact that she'd run like she was being chased by a pack of wild dogs when things had gotten too intense was a good indication that she wasn't interested in exploring what could have happened if they had not been interrupted. He needed to remember that.

"So," Mason asked, deciding that small talk was necessary to break through the awkward silence. "Is the gas gauge on your car broken?"

She turned to him and swiped at her cheek, and he realized she'd had her head averted to block her tears from his view.

Shit.

He really didn't want to know what had caused them. He was in deep enough as it was.

"No," she said. "I just have a bad habit of running on empty." She choked out a teary laugh. "Don't tell Kiera about this. She and Callie harp on me constantly, with good reason."

"Your secret's safe," he said as he pulled up

to the first traffic light at the edge of Maplesville proper. The light turned green and he switched to the right lane so that he could turn at the next light. Then he remembered that she no longer lived in the huge white house on Dogwood Drive that she'd shared with Eric.

"Uh, Jada, where exactly are you living now?"

She hesitated for a moment before saying, "The apartment building at the corner of Willow and Fir."

Mason shot her a quick glance. There wasn't necessarily any part of Maplesville that was unsavory, but some parts were definitely less desirable than others. To go from living in one of Maplesville's most established neighborhoods to the part of town where she now lived must have taken some major mental adjusting.

When they pulled into the parking lot of her building, Jada didn't give him a chance to turn the car off before she was out the door. She had the back door open and was pulling out her travel case by the time he rounded the car.

"I've got it," she said when he went for the case.

Mason ignored her, plucking the handle from her fingers. "Lead the way," he said.

"You don't have to do this. The fact that you brought me home is enough."

Mason pitched his head back and sighed. "Damn, woman, do you get some twisted

—

77

pleasure out of being this stubborn?"

Her bottom lip trembled with a tremulous smile. She hunched her shoulders, as if to say "Fine, have it your way" and led the way to her second floor apartment. Once they arrived at the door, she turned and reached for the bag. This time he let her take it.

"Thanks again for doing this," she said.

"You keep thanking me as if I would have left you on the side of the road."

"I know, I know," she said. "It's just that you're being so nice...and you...you don't even like me."

She dissolved into a mess of tears again, dropping the bag and covering her face with both hands.

Mason cursed.

He snatched the keys from her fingers and tried out three before he was able to unlock the front door. He shoved the travel case inside, then wrapped an arm around her shoulders, ushering her into the apartment. As he guided her to the sofa, he looked around, astounded at how damn tiny this place was. A claustrophobic would go insane after two minutes in here.

Once Jada was seated, Mason stooped in front of her and used his thumbs to wipe the moisture from her face.

"Hey, hey," he whispered, smoothing her hair back. "Didn't anyone ever tell you there's no crying in G-Swirl Vibrator sales?"

She choked out a laugh, brushing at her damp cheeks.

Mason tipped her chin up and looked her in the eyes. "You okay?"

"No." She sniffed, shaking her head. "I hate admitting it, but I'm so not okay."

His chest tightened with sympathy. He'd never seen her like this before. The Jada Dangerfield he knew was spunky and spirited. To see her lose it like this made him ache for her.

She held her palms up and hunched her shoulders. "I just don't understand how someone who hates me can be so nice, while someone I was married to just a year ago treats me like dirt."

Mason grimaced. "I don't hate you, Jada. Please, stop saying that."

"But, you do," she insisted. "We hate each other; always have. That's just how we roll." She said it so matter-of-factly Mason couldn't help but laugh.

"Do you want some water?" he asked.

She nodded.

He walked two steps into her kitchen — it was literally two steps away — and poured a glass of water from one of those water-filtration pitchers. He brought her the glass, then went into the bathroom in search of a washcloth.

He grabbed one from a wire shelf that stood over the toilet and soaked it with warm water. As he rung out the washcloth, Mason caught sight of something black and lacy sitting on top of the heap of laundry in the clothes hamper.

"Holy shit," he choked out.

He braced his hands against the sides of the sink and sucked in a deep breath. How in the hell did he end up in Jada Dangerfield's bathroom, just inches from her black lace panties? How in the hell was he supposed to go back out there and not picture her wearing something similar? Maybe in blue? Hot pink?

Damn, but he didn't need this right now. Neither did Jada. Something had happened to her tonight that had rubbed her emotions raw. What she needed from him was that same tender care she'd given his injured arm yesterday. She did *not* need him obsessing over her underwear. Her possibly hot pink underwear.

Mason squeezed his eyes tight and did his best to pull himself together, despite the lust that continued to rush through his veins like a runaway freight train.

He re-wet the washcloth and rung it out again before heading back to the living room.

Jada sat with her feet tucked underneath her, both hands wrapped around the glass of water. Mason handed her the washcloth. He'd had all intentions of wiping the tears from her face for her, but now every instinct advised he maintain his distance.

Well, as much distance as possible in this tiny ass apartment.

One part of him — the reasonable, practical part — was telling him to get out now. He'd done his good deed for the day, going above and beyond what could be expected. But when he caught sight of her, looking so vulnerable, her emotions so exposed, his reasonable side took a backseat to the man who had been tasked since boyhood with protecting the women in his life.

Mason sat next to her on the sofa. He fought the impulse to reach for her.

"So," he started. "Do you want to talk about what had you crying your eyes out on the side of the highway? It can't be because you ran out of gas."

She shook her head.

"Then what is it, Jada? Did your asshole of an ex-husband do something to you?"

She tipped her head to the side, her brows arching with curiosity. "Why have you always hated Eric so much?"

"Because he's always been an asshole and a bully," Mason answered. "What did he do to you?"

Her bottom lip trembled. "He got his wife pregnant," she said, before dissolving into tears again.

Mason wasn't sure what to do with that one. It would have been a lot easier to defend her if Eric had called her a bad name or made some other asshole-like move.

"Uh, okay," he said.

Jada put her hand up, staving off further comment, which was a good thing because he had nothing.

"I'm just having a moment," she said. "I know it's stupid, but I can't help it." She twisted toward him on the sofa, putting both feet up and sliding her knees up to her chest. "His new wife showed up at the party I threw in Covington this evening. Can you believe that? I've given nearly a dozen Naughty Nights parties in and around Maplesville, yet she shows up to one that's an hour away.

"Anyway," she continued with a dismissive wave. "I chalked it up to one of those crazy coincidences, and decided to roll with it. I was doing just fine until she announced that she was pregnant. After that I just lost it. I locked myself in the bathroom and cried like a baby."

She pressed her balled fist against her trembling lips, but she wasn't able to stop the two tears that streamed down her face.

He'd known her over seventeen years, and had never come even close to seeing her so vulnerable. Jada was a spitfire. She was bold and brash and she didn't take shit from anybody.

But right now she was hurting, and it was painful to watch.

Despite his better judgment, Mason palmed her knee, giving it a slight squeeze. "It'll be okay," he said. "You're allowed to go on a crying jag every now and then."

"It's just…I don't know…like a slap in the face." She sniffed. "I wanted a baby so badly, and we tried so many times to get pregnant."

Okay, he was not up to hearing about Jada and Eric and their many attempts to procreate.

"I know it's petty, but I just hate that Eric is getting his baby and I'm not." She swiped at even more tears. Mason was surprised she had any left. "Oh, God, why am I talking about this with you? You, of all people!" She groaned, wrapping her arms around her legs and dropping her head to her knees.

"Hey," Mason said, unable to keep the affront from his voice. "What's that supposed to mean? Me, of all people?"

She lifted her head and shot him one of those sardonic looks he'd come to know so well from her. "You've been great tonight, but we both know the real deal. You've barely tolerated me from the moment you met me."

Mason just stared at her for several moments, a small smile tilting up his lips. "You really are clueless, aren't you?"

"See, that's what I mean." She threw her palms up. "You think I'm a dumb, clueless, airhead cheerleader."

Mason's brow drew inward with censure. "You beat out Callie for valedictorian of your high school class and finished college and graduate school in five years. I have never thought you were dumb, clueless, or an airhead.

As for the cheerleader…well, you wore the uniform."

And drove him crazy every time he saw her in it.

The corner of her mouth hitched in an impish grin. "I guess I can't argue with that. I did indeed wear the uniform," she said.

The easy smile he was able to draw from her made him feel as if he could leap tall buildings, grab clouds from the sky with his hands, do just about anything he desired.

Mason leaned over and captured her chin in his fingers. "And I told you before, I don't hate you. I've never hated you, Jada."

Her skeptical expression wrung another chuckle from him. "I called you clueless because after all these years, you never figured out that I had the biggest crush on you when you first moved to Maplesville."

She jerked her chin out of his hold. "*What?*"

Mason shrugged. "I did."

"You couldn't stand me when I first moved here. In fact, you said those exact words to me on more than one occasion."

"I know," Mason admitted. "What I probably should have said was that I couldn't stand how quickly you fell for Eric's bullshit, like every other girl in school. It was so predictable. But when I saw how hard he fell for *you*, it made it even worse, because I knew there had to be something special about you. It irritated the hell out of me that of all the guys you could have chosen, you chose him."

"You really don't like him, do you?"

Mason shook his head. "Never did. We got in a fight on the first day of second grade after I found him picking on a couple of kindergarteners. We've butted heads ever since." He peered over at her. "I truly don't know how you spent all those years with him. It's as if you're blind to the type of person he is."

"*Was* blind," she corrected. "My eyes are open now." Jada blew out a tired breath. "You know what really gets to me? The fact that he's winning. I hate it."

"He's winning?"

"Yes!" She pounded her fist with every item she ticked off. "He got all the money, he's married again, and now he's getting a baby. And what do I have? I'm unemployed, living in this shoebox, and I haven't had sex with something that doesn't require batteries in over a year."

He couldn't do anything about the first two, but Mason had to stop himself from offering to change the status on her third issue.

Jada rubbed her temples and let out a groan. "God, when did I become this whiny complainer? I hate complainers." She shook her head and huffed out a humorless laugh. "I just don't know how I ended up here. I was living the fairytale. Married to my high school sweetheart, living in one of the biggest houses in town, working at a great job. And then…poof. It all came crashing down."

"But you're still here," Mason pointed out. He reached over and tucked a lock of wavy hair behind her ear, letting his hand linger. Could her skin be any softer? "You realize that what you've been through this past year would break some people, don't you, Jada? But you've managed to keep it together. Well, other than that little bonfire incident Kiera told me about," he added with a grin.

She winced and dropped her head to her knees again.

"All joking aside, you should be proud of the way you've handled this. Despite the blows you've taken, you're still standing."

"I guess you're right," she muttered. "I'm alone and unemployed, but at least I'm still standing."

"But you're not unemployed. What about this new…what did you call it? Consulting business?"

She shrugged. "That's just a side gig to tide me over until I can find a real job." She glanced up at him, a wry grin tilting her lips. "Maplesville isn't all that big. I'll eventually run out of people to sell G-Swirl Vibrators to."

Relief flowed through him at the sight of the humor sparkling in her eyes again. Sadness still echoed in her subdued voice, but Mason sensed she'd broken through a threshold tonight. The pleasure he derived from knowing that he'd played a role in helping her get to this point was intoxicating.

Just one more reason why he should get the hell out of here.

His work was done. In fact, he'd accomplished more than he'd set out to. He'd provided a shoulder for her to cry on, an understanding ear to listen to her list of problems.

But he didn't want to leave her. He wanted to sit right here for as long as she would allow. So, in a move that was astoundingly contradictory to his usual mode of operation, Mason put a muzzle on the voice of reason resonating in his head and encouraged Jada to keep talking.

"How's the job search going?" he asked.

"Well, I'm still unemployed, which should give you some indication." She told him about a public relations position she'd applied for that she considered her ideal job. "It's with this organization that oversees several non-profits around the New Orleans metro area. I would love to work for a company that actually does some good in the world."

"What's the organization?" Mason asked, hoping she would name one in particular.

"The Fortier Foundation," she answered.

That was the one.

Mason had to stop himself from smiling.

Maybe he *could* help solve one of the issues plaguing her. He made a mental note to make a call tomorrow.

"The job market is pretty competitive, so I'm not holding my breath," Jada continued. "I'm just grateful to have the Naughty Nights parties providing some income."

"How did you get into throwing these parties anyway?" Mason asked, settling back on the sofa and draping an arm across the top of it.

"I saw an advertisement in one of those Internet pop-up ads."

He tipped his head to the side, his eyes narrowing. "Exactly what were you looking at in order to get that kind of pop-up?"

Her forehead furrowed. "What do you mean?"

"I'm just thinking about the way Internet advertising works. Your web browser stores cookies based on the various websites you visit, and use that info to target their ads. So, what kind of websites were you looking at in order to get pop-up advertising for erotic toys?"

Her mouth opened and closed as her light brown cheeks instantly reddened. She groaned, burying her face in her hands.

A laugh rumbled from deep in his belly.

"Oh, shut up, Mason," she mumbled from behind her hands.

"God, you're adorable."

She spread her fingers, peeking at him

through the openings. "You just called me adorable."

"Because you are," he murmured, narrowing the distance between them. Mason halted for just a moment, giving her the chance to object.

She didn't. She just stared at his lips, her chest rising and falling softly with her measured breaths.

Mason leaned forward, finally touching his lips to hers.

That first touch was everything he'd expected, yet more than he could have ever imagined. Her mouth was soft, and pliant, and so damn delicious it was like a decadent dessert at the end of a fine meal. Mason traced his tongue along the seam of her lips, concentrating on every nuance: the bow shape that dipped in the center, the subtle poutiness of her bottom lip, and the incredible, velvety feel of them as she yielded to his kiss.

Her lips parted slightly, and he took full advantage, licking his way into her mouth, plying her with firm, deliberate strokes. He caressed the inside of her mouth, acquiring knowledge of every corner, relishing its taste and texture. Mason's skin prickled with want as he cradled the back of her head and held her in place while his tongue advanced and retreated, gently thrusting, steadily devouring.

Jada's tongue took a tentative surge forward,

wringing a groan from deep in his throat.

His body reacted predictably to the feel of her supple, exquisite lips against his, the organ in his lap burgeoning with arousal. His skin grew tight; his muscles tensing with the flood of need coursing through him. His fingers massaged the back of her head as his other hand crept up her side. He hesitated for just a moment before covering her breast with his palm.

A tortured moan tore out of Mason's throat as the feel of her rock hard nipple branded his palm. He squeezed and rubbed her breast, committing the sensation to memory.

This had been a fantasy for far too long. He'd dreamed of what Jada would taste like, how it would feel to touch her like this. It was everything he'd imagined and more.

And, God, how he wanted more.

Which was why he needed to stop.

Her emotions were still raw, all of her vulnerabilities still too exposed. He refused to go any further knowing that she was at a disadvantage.

Mason indulged in one final sweep of her mouth, then immediately decided it wasn't enough and stroked his tongue again, savoring every drop of her flavor just in case this was the one and only time he would get to experience it. With the strength of will one called upon only once in a lifetime, he forced himself to pull away. His tongue instantly regretted the absence of the moist warmth it had been enjoying a second ago.

Jada's eyes slowly open. They were a bit dazed, as if she wasn't sure what had just happened.

He knew exactly what had happened, and damn if he wasn't seconds from begging her to let it happen again. Mason braced his hands on his thighs and pushed himself up, the need to escape temptation reluctant, but necessary.

"I should go," he said. "Will you lock the door behind me?"

She nodded, wrapping her arms around her knees again. "I'll get it in a minute," she said.

Mason stopped with his hand on the doorknob and glanced back at her. "Will you be okay?"

Another nod. "I will," she said, her voice thready. "Mason," she called when he opened the door. He looked back. "Thank you for not really hating me all these years."

He grinned. "You're welcome. Good night, Jada," he said before shutting the door behind him.

Once in his car, Mason strapped himself into his seat and turned over the ignition. He gripped the steering wheel, glancing at the time illuminated on the dash. It was nearly eleven p.m. Still, he let his car idle for another ten minutes while he stared at Jada's second-floor apartment and tried to convince himself not to walk back up there and knock on her door.

Chapter Five

Reclining in his desk chair, Mason flipped through the ledger that had been delivered by special courier this morning. He had an afternoon meeting scheduled with the CFO of Marshall Construction, the first client he'd landed when he began working at Olivier, Broussard and Polk fresh out of law school.

It was a good thing he knew Marshall's finances inside and out, because his concentration was for shit today.

Mason tossed the ledger on the desk, swiveled his chair around, and stared at the view of the Mississippi River afforded by his office's floor-to-ceiling windows. He tapped a capped pen against his lips, his eyes drawn to a line of colorful barges drifting along the calm water.

As he absently observed the lazy river traffic, Mason allowed his mind to fully embrace the memory of last night, when he'd captured Jada's lips in the kind of kiss that could distract a normally focused workaholic from focusing on anything else.

If he hadn't put an end to their kiss, he had

---

no doubt they would have ended up naked on her tiny couch. He and Jada. Naked. Together.

Shit. He wanted that so badly his skin tightened just at the thought.

He'd done the right thing in leaving. The morally-sound, gentlemanly part of him knew that taking advantage of her weakened defenses would have been wrong. But there was another part that wanted to say to hell with being a gentleman; the part that was dying to finally fulfill all the fantasies he'd indulged in over the years.

"Thank goodness you didn't," Mason murmured to himself. Exploiting her vulnerability would have made him no better than that piece of shit she'd been married to.

Just thinking about Eric and the way Jada cried over him last night made Mason want to pummel the wall with his fist, the way he'd pummeled Eric's face back when they were kids. He'd left out of a sense of integrity last night, but he realized that nothing he did or didn't do could ever be as bad as what Eric had done to her. Eric had broken her spirit, and Mason was all too willing to help her mend it back together.

But who's to say Jada would even welcome his help in moving past her ex?

He may have secretly wanted her all these years, but it was obvious she'd had no clue, which meant her decade-long dislike of him had been real. Was it even worth the effort to try and convince her that they should bury the animosity that had always existed between them?

He ran his hands down his face as he pitched his head back against the chair's leather headrest.

He had no idea how, or even *if*, he should try to move forward with Jada. Maybe there *was* no moving forward. Maybe last night was all he would ever get. Maybe that one amazing kiss would have to last him a lifetime.

Whether Jada chose to acknowledge what had passed between them last night or not, Mason knew there was one thing he still wanted to do for her. He reached for his phone and scrolled through the names until he found Selena Pareja. He dialed it and was informed by an automated recording that the number was no longer in service.

Damn, had it been that *long since he'd called?*

He Googled The Fortier Foundation and dialed the number. He asked to speak to Selena, and was put through moments after he told the receptionist his name.

"Mason Coleman," Selena's smooth voice came over the line. "It's been a while."

"Apparently," he said. "I tried you on your cell, but the number's changed."

"I lost my phone last year while in Tokyo. I didn't bother sending you the new number since you hadn't called in a while." Mason knew her pregnant pause was by design. "So, to what do I owe this call?"

If this were anyone else Mason would hesitate before asking for a favor for another woman, but Selena was like him, a professional. She wouldn't allow hurt feelings to get in the way of business.

What was he talking about? Selena wouldn't allow hurt feelings, period.

He told her about Jada, sharing what he knew of her years at the oil refinery where she'd worked as a PR representative, and about her enthusiasm for the job with Selena's organization.

"She's very interested in the work The Fortier Foundation is doing," he said.

"Mason, you are the only man bold enough to ask his ex-girlfriend to hire his current girlfriend."

"She's not my girlfriend, just a longtime friend of my sister's," he said. "And I'm calling because I know she would be perfect for the job. I'm not saying you have to hire her—"

"Because you know I won't hire her if she's not qualified."

"She is," he said. "But I'm just asking that you pay close attention to her résumé. If I were you I'd call her in for an interview sooner rather than later. I have no doubt she'll be snatched up by an employer soon."

"Thanks for the tip," Selena said. After

another pause she added, "I won't bother asking you to dinner because I know you're a one-woman man. And, despite your denial, I know this Jada has to be more than just a friend. You wouldn't stick your neck out otherwise. I'll talk to you later, Mason."

Once he'd disconnected the call, Mason tapped the phone against his lips, contemplating Selena's words. Just a week ago, Jada would not have fallen under the classification of friend. To consider her *more* than a friend?

"Stop making a big deal out of it," he muttered. It wasn't as if he'd gone out of his way; he'd made a simple call.

Mason set the cell phone on his desk and returned to the ledger he'd been reviewing. A minute later, his desk phone buzzed.

"Mr. Coleman, it's Dudley Cook," his assistant announced through the speaker.

Mason's eyelids slid shut against the headache that instantly sprouted behind his eyes. He was not in the mood for dealing with Oscar Davis's cutthroat CPA today.

"Mr. Cook," Mason answered.

"What's the word on Vanuatu?" the other man asked.

"Dudley, I already explained the risk of setting up a tax haven in Vanuatu."

"And I told you that Mr. Davis is willing to take the risk. I asked you to look into Seychelles, also. Have you made any progress on that?"

"Seychelles has the same risk as Vanuatu."

As Cook went on a rant, Mason picked up the stress ball Kiera had given him as a gag gift for his birthday last year, and clutched it in his fist. Lately, he used the stress ball more than the tennis racket she'd intended as his real gift.

"I never said it was illegal," Mason interrupted. "I said it's a gray area. Very gray. The IRS is looking at offshore accounts much more closely than they have in the past. Mr. Davis is barely paying eleven-percent right now. If he goes down to an even lower rate he's essentially putting a bull's-eye on his back."

"Again, it's a risk he's willing to take. Now, if you're not up for this, find us someone in the firm who is," Cook said before abruptly ending the call.

Mason pitched the stress ball across the office and pushed away from his desk.

Making partner was the next step in the chronology of the goals he'd set for himself years ago. The current partners were paying close attention to the Davis account. If he wasn't careful he could very well be the snag that caused his own plans to unravel.

But if the only way to a partnership was by compromising his principals, did he really want it?

"Dammit," Mason whispered.

He knew exactly what his conscience was telling him to do, but he was starting to question if always doing the right thing was holding him back.

***

"Okay, Kiera, enough with the half-assed explanations. It's time for you to tell us what's going on with you."

"Here, here," Jada said, tipping her goblet of merlot in Callie's direction. "You've been acting shady for over a week. It's time for you to spill."

Kiera groaned. "God, can't a person have one tiny little detail of their lives to themselves?"

"No," Jada and Callie said in unison.

Kiera sent them both a nasty look, but Jada shrugged it off. It wasn't as if she'd never gotten that look from her before.

The three of them had been best friends since their sophomore year of high school, and had remained close, despite going to separate colleges. But, eventually, life started to get in the way. As Kiera's catering business took off, and Callie's veterinary practice expanded, they found themselves going months without seeing each other for more than a few minutes, usually when they ran into each other at the grocery store, or the dry cleaners.

These monthly get-togethers arose out of necessity when Callie's world imploded after her husband revealed that he was leaving her for his younger, pregnant girlfriend. Being an only child whose parents had been killed while she was still in college, Callie had needed them desperately.

When Eric followed suit, leaving Jada in the same predicament Callie had been in, they continued their get-togethers. At least Eric had waited a little longer before he got his new girl pregnant.

Poor Kiera's love life had always warranted massive amounts of alcohol, despite her being the optimist of the group. At this point, Jada wasn't sure Kiera was even looking for love anymore.

Unless…

"Is this about a man?" Jada asked. "Please don't tell me you accepted Garrett's friendship request on Facebook."

"No," Kiera said. "I blocked him. I even blocked his number from my cell phone and the phone at the kitchen. This has nothing to do with Garrett."

"Then what is it?" Callie asked, passing around the plate of double fudge, dark chocolate caramel brownies that should be declared illegal in all fifty states. Jada was sure the calories in just one was enough to kill a small dog.

Kiera groaned again. She lay prone across the cushioned armchair in Callie's living room, her feet dangling over one armrest while her back bowed over the other. Jada tucked her feet underneath her, studying her friend from her spot on the loveseat.

"We're only asking because we're concerned," Jada told her.

"And nosy," Kiera returned.

"That, too." Callie topped off her wineglass. "You know we're here to help. But we need to know what's going on so that we'll know *how* to help."

Kiera sat upright and folded her legs underneath her. "Fine. I know neither of you will stop until you get all the gory details, anyway."

"Wait, just how gory are the details?" Callie asked. "Do I need to uncork another bottle before you begin?"

"No, I think we're good with what we have." Kiera took a deep breath. "Okay, remember when I told you guys that I wanted to branch out with Catering by Kiera?"

"You mentioned that you were considering getting a food truck to take into New Orleans."

"Yeah, well, when I looked into it, I found out that they can run upwards of a hundred thousand."

"Dollars!" Jada screeched. "For an ice cream truck with a stove?"

"They're a lot more than ice cream trucks with stoves." Kiera drawled. She ticked items off on her fingers. "They're fully wired, they require a ventilation system, a three-compartment sink. Basically everything you would need for a brick and mortar restaurant. And all that stuff has to be up to code."

"So, will you have to put off buying the food truck for a while? Is that why you've been so off lately?" Jada asked as she reached for another brownie.

Kiera released another sigh. "I bought a food truck. From Craigslist."

Jada dropped the brownie. "Craigslist?"

"Sight unseen," Kiera said. She covered her face with both hands and groaned. "I know. I know. It was the stupidest thing I could have done, but it was such a good deal, and the pictures they had up on the website looked good enough."

"How much did you pay?" Callie asked.

"Twenty-thousand. Cash."

"Holy shit, Kiera!" Jada sat upright.

"Did they falsify the ad?" Callie asked. "Because there should be some type of recourse if they did."

"No, no." She shook her head. "The seller warned that the truck needed some work. I just didn't realize how *much* work. And they definitely took the most advantageous shots of the truck."

"Do you have any idea how much it'll take to get it up to code?" Callie asked.

"The estimate I've gotten is another twenty-thousand, at least."

"Holy shit, Kiera!" Jada said again.

"You want to add something else to the conversation other than 'holy shit'?"

"I'm sorry," Jada said. "I knew something was bothering you, I just wasn't expecting something like this. What do you plan to do?"

"If I don't get the truck up and running, the twenty-thousand I paid for it will be all for nothing. And I really want to get this new aspect of Catering by Kiera off the ground, before Jazz Fest, if possible."

"Was the twenty-thousand the last of the money from your dad's life insurance?" Callie asked.

Kiera nodded. "I tried getting a loan at the bank, but they're asking me to put my business up as collateral. I can't take that chance."

"No way," Callie said. "I'll loan you the money."

"I don't want it. That's the kind of money that can break up friendships."

"Don't be ridiculous, Kiera."

She put her hand up. "I'm not even entertaining the idea, Callie."

"What about Mason?" Jada asked. Her skin got a little flush just saying his name. She was pathetic.

"No, no, no," Kiera said with a vehement shake of her head. "I don't want him to know about any of this. Mason has been bailing me out my entire life. This is *my* predicament. I'll figure out a way to make it work."

"I understand how that is," Jada said. She and Kiera were alike in that they both had relied on family for virtually everything. Jada was proud of the stand her friend was taking. They were growing up. Look at them.

"Are you sure, Kiera?" Callie asked.

"Yes. Now, let's change the subject. *Please*. I'm tired of thinking about my financial woes." She turned to Jada. "What about you? You had that Naughty Nights party over in Covington. How did it go?"

Jada looked over at Callie. "You may want to pop the cork on that other bottle of wine."

"Uh, oh," Callie said. "What happened?"

Jada relayed the details of the party, explaining how she endured listening to Nikki talk about her and Eric's sex life. When she told them about Nikki's pregnancy, both Kiera and Callie came over and enveloped her in a hug. They knew the affect that kind of news had on her spirit. It was just one of the reasons she was closer to these two women than she was to her own sister.

"And, to top it all off, I ran out of gas on my way home."

Kiera drew back from their group hug and raised an accusatory brow. "You know I have to say it, right?"

"You don't *have* to," Jada pointed out. Kiera's brows nudged higher. "Fine," Jada said.

"I told you so," Kiera pronounced.

"There, you feel better?"

"Much," her friend returned while Callie laughed.

"It actually turned out to be a pretty good night," Jada continued. "A knight in shining armor came to my rescue."

"Really?" Callie asked. "Anyone we know?"

A knock on the door drew their attention. Before Callie could answer it, the door opened and in walked Stefan Sutherland, Callie's boyfriend of four months.

"Hello, ladies," Stefan greeted. The hunky ex-Navy pilot had come to Maplesville back in November to take care of his nephew while his twin sister, an Army nurse, was deployed to Afghanistan. His and Callie's worlds collided when Stefan brought a stray cat he'd rescued from a ditch to Callie's animal clinic.

Callie jumped up from the couch and ran over to Stefan, wrapping her arms around his neck. The two proceeded to suck face like a couple of teenagers.

"Oh, give me a break," Kiera muttered. "I thought it was romantic when they first started dating, but now it just makes me want to smack both of them."

After her face-sucking session with Mason, Jada didn't think it wise to comment. She also wasn't sure she was ready to let Kiera know about what transpired between her and Mason. She was still trying to evaluate and absorb exactly what had happened between them herself.

Still holding hands, Stefan and Callie joined them in the living room.

"Sorry to interrupt the Girls Night In party, but I promised Callie I'd bring over her laptop as soon as I was done with it. It now has twice as much memory."

"Handsome and handy," Kiera said with an overly dramatic sigh. "Callie Webber, if I didn't love you so much I would hate you, you lucky wench."

Stefan laughed. "I'll leave you ladies to your fun."

"Actually, I'm going to leave with you," Jada said. "I have another job interview in the morning. I need to turn in early."

"Is it with the firm in New Orleans?" Callie asked.

"No, they haven't called. This one is in Picayune. I'll settle for it until I can find something more permanent."

"Hey," Kiera called. "You never told us the name of your knight in shining armor."

Jada stopped just inside the door Stefan held open for her and looked back over her shoulder.

"Remember when you asked if a person can have one tiny detail of their lives to themselves? I just decided they can."

She stuck her tongue out at them, laughing at the irate shouts from Kiera and Callie that followed her out the door.

Chapter Six

As Jada drove up to the curb in front of Mason's house, she tried to calm the nerves that were ping-ponging inside her belly. She'd been both dreading and anticipating returning to his home with equal amounts of anxiety and excitement. She knew for a fact that he wasn't even at home, and she was *still* on edge.

It had been a long time since she'd had to contend with these types of feelings, and it exposed just how bland her marriage had become. The fact that Eric had not elicited anything even remotely as arousing within her in at least the past five years revealed much.

Was it the newness of it? Or the unexpectedness, maybe?

Nothing on the face of this planet or the next could have been more unexpected than the kiss she and Mason shared the other night. And his admission that he'd had a secret crush on her years ago? Unexpected didn't cover the half of it.

Jada walked over to the side of the garage and felt inside the drain pipe for the key Kiera had told her would be hidden there. She'd left the alarm off, not telling Mason, who would have probably gone ballistic over that.

Jada grabbed her travel bag and another bag of decorations she'd picked up and went into the house.

She deposited the bags on the dining room table where the other things she'd bought for Kiera's party still sat. She told herself that she should just get right to work getting ready for the party, but Kiera wouldn't get here for at least another hour, and it wasn't going to take her *that* long to string a couple of heart-shaped banners around the room. She had Mason's house to herself for a little while, why not satisfy the curiosity that had been bombarding her for the past couple of days?

Jada hugged her arms around her upper body as she moved around the large, pentagon-shaped living room. The two sides on the left both featured arched entrances to the dining room and the kitchen. The far right side held a massive fireplace made of slate stone in varying shades of gray and soft brown.

Mason had always been very no-nonsense, so it didn't surprise her that while the house was tastefully decorated, it was also minimalist. There were no knick knacks cluttering the shelves, no collection of sports memorabilia, or car magazines, or any of the other stuff Eric used to have around their home.

However, there was a slim, glass buffet table

that held several framed photographs. It seemed so homey when compared to the austere feel of the rest of the space.

Jada ambled over to the buffet and perused the collection of pictures. There was a photograph of his parents on their wedding day. Jada picked the picture up, laughing at the massive afro on the groom's head. The couple had to stand at least a foot apart just so Cecilia Coleman, who looked as radiant as ever, could be seen.

As she studied the photograph, Jada was struck by how closely Mason resembled his father. She picked up a picture of father and son in fishing gear. Mason couldn't have been more than six years old. He was holding up a tiny fish, but by the proud smile on his face one would think he'd reeled in a marlin. In all the years she'd known him, Jada doubted she'd ever seen Mason so cheerful and carefree as he was in this picture.

A gentle ache echoed in her heart for the young boy who had been forced to become the man of the house at such an early age. He shouldered so much responsibility, but in all the years she'd known him, he never complained.

She set the picture back on the table and took a slow turn, her gaze encompassing the entire room. Jada eyed the smaller arched entryway that led to the hallway, which she knew led to his bedroom and home office. But she felt as if she'd violated his privacy enough; she would not intrude more than she had already.

Instead, she gathered the bags of decorations she'd bought for the party and began putting them up around the living room.

Twenty minutes later, Jada heard the smooth rumble of a car engine and the distinct whirl of the garage door opening. Her heart started beating ten times faster, but she forced herself to keep her attention centered on the curtain of cascading foil hearts she was hanging across the entryway between the living room and kitchen.

Moments later, she heard the door that led from the garage opening.

The sound of Mason's footsteps against the hardwood floor as he walked toward her pounded in her ears…and in her blood, causing it to rush through her veins like a river in spring.

"Hi," he greeted from behind her.

Jada glanced over her shoulder, trying to act nonchalant. "Hi."

How could a single syllable come out so damn breathy?

Another few awkward moments passed.

"So, Kiera's party is tonight, huh?"

"It starts at seven."

She turned back to the curtain, and was unbelievably grateful when he took the hint and headed toward the hallway leading to the back of the house.

She just didn't know how to handle this new, unexpected turn in their relationship. She had never been at a loss for words when it came to speaking to Mason. It's just that usually her words came in the form of cheap shots or heated arguments. How were they supposed to act now that he'd had his tongue in her mouth?

Her stomach clenched as warmth flooded her lower region. Jada just suffered through it. It took too much energy to fight the visceral reaction she experienced whenever she thought about that kiss.

She moved the step-stool ladder to the entryway that led to the dining room and began hanging a matching glittery curtain along the top.

"Jada, we need to talk about what happened the other night," Mason said from behind her.

She yelped, twisting around and nearly losing her balance. She hadn't even heard his approach.

"Hold on there," he said, steadying her with both hands at her waist. "I think one ladder accident a month is enough."

Her skin tingled where he touched her, despite the layer of clothing between her waist and his fingers. She climbed down from the ladder, noticing he was wearing only socks, which explained why she hadn't heard him walking up to her.

She folded her arms across her chest and nervously moistened her suddenly dry lips. "What is it about the other night that you want to discuss?"

Mason stuck one hand in the pocket of his black pants, while he brought the other up to massage the back of his neck.

"Well, there's a lot we can discuss, but the part when our tongues got to know each other better is what's been on my mind lately."

Jada thanked God that her arms were already covering her chest, because her nipples instantly sprouted to attention.

"That should at least warrant a conversation, don't you think?" Mason asked.

She cleared her throat, giving herself time to think. "Circumstances being what they were, it's understandable that…that something like that occurred."

His brow dipped low. "So, that's your take on it?"

"Mason, it was just a kiss."

Annoyance flashed across his face. "Can any kiss between the two of us be considered *just* a kiss?"

"For God's sake, Mason. We've been at each other's throats since the day we met. Why would you think one kiss would make any difference whatsoever?"

The intensity of his stare as he regarded her with those deep brown eyes set off a bevy of nervous flutters along her skin. He took a step forward, closing the distance between them. When he spoke, his voice was low and husky, in a mesmerizing, breath-stealing kind of way.

"You want to know why I think one kiss makes a difference?" He held his palm up. "Because I can still feel where your nipple was pressed up against my hand. The feeling won't go away."

Just like that, her nipples hardened even more. Jada hugged herself tight, her eyes falling closed. "Mason, what do you want from me?"

"I want you to acknowledge what happened the other night." He captured her chin and tilted her head up. "Did you ever stop to wonder if maybe all this time there's been more than just negative feelings between us? Maybe there's been something else beneath the surface that neither of us were brave enough to admit to."

"I was married for the majority of the time we've known each other," she reminded him in a voice so faint she could barely hear it herself.

He drew his fingers along her jawline, caressing her skin, his touch achingly tender. His other hand cradled the back of her head, his fingers massaging her scalp with gentle circles.

Holding her steady, Mason whispered, "You're not anymore."

Jada braced herself in the seconds before his lips touched hers, but the impact still hit her with the force of a meteor crashing into the

Earth.

Mason wasted no time, his tongue moving with an insistence much like he'd shown at her apartment. He masterfully took charge of her mouth, pushing past the seam of her lips and plying the inside with his tongue. He brought his other hand up and held her head steady as he licked and sucked and tasted, eliciting all manner of sensations in her, causing them to resonate throughout her body.

The feeble protest she considered voicing was no match for the part of her that demanded she enjoy every single bit of his kiss for however long she could. Jada angled her head to the side and soaked in this feeling, loving the way he took his time, nipping at her bottom lip, pulling it between his teeth before sucking on it.

His lips seared a path along her jawline. Jada angled her head back, giving him room as he kissed his way down her neck, nibbling and lapping at her skin.

Mason backed her up against the dining room table. With one hand he swiped the sex toys and decorations cluttering the table to the floor, then he grabbed her by the hips and sat her atop the polished wood, stepping between her spread legs and fitting his body against hers.

Jada ran her hands up the silky softness of his button-down shirt, marveling at the contours underneath. She pulled his shirt from the waistband of his pants and pushed her hands up, loving the feel of his skin against her fingers.

"God, Mason! Are you kidding me?" she asked as her head fell back.

"What?" he murmured against her neck. The moist tip of his tongue trailed along the base of her throat, triggering a maelstrom of butterflies to flitter in the pit of her stomach.

"All this time." She gasped. "You and this tongue have been here all this time."

Jada felt the rumble of his deep laugh against her skin and it set off yet another ripple of sensations in her belly. And lower.

He brought his mouth back to hers, while his hands swooped down and cradled her ass. Mason pulled her more tightly against him, until their bodies were flush.

Jada let out a soft whimper at the undeniable hardness pressing against her. Her body was on fire, every inch of her skin igniting with excited little bursts of heat. She wanted more of that hardness. She wanted to feel it inside her, buried deep, while the muscled contours of his chest flattened her breasts.

Good God, how she wanted that!

The sound of a car engine rumbling outside wrenched her out of her pleasure-soaked fantasy.

"Mason, stop," she said against his lips. "That's probably Kiera." She pushed against his chest. "Mason, Kiera's here."

"So," he said.

She pointed to his crotch. "Do you really want your little sister to see you like this?"

Oh, God. She'd *caused that.*

She was responsible for giving *Mason Coleman* an erection to rival any erection she'd ever seen.

"Oh, my God. Mason, what are we doing?"

A sexy smile tilted up his lips. "If I have to explain it, Eric really wasn't doing his job."

He pressed a swift kiss to her lips and headed for the back hallway. Mere seconds later, Kiera walked through the door.

Jada hopped off the dining room table and straightened her clothes. She combed her fingers through her wavy, natural curls.

"I've got the…snacks," Kiera trailed off as she walked into the dining room carrying a tray. She gestured to the mess on the floor. "What happened here?"

Jada waved her off. "I tripped and knocked all of this off the table trying to break my fall. You know how much of a klutz I am." She stooped down and started picking up the items Mason had swept off the table before he'd lifted her onto it.

"Did you hit yourself when you fell?"

Jada looked up. "What?"

Kiera gestured to her own collarbone. "You've got something red forming there. Did you bruise yourself?"

That wasn't a bruise. That was the result of

Mason sucking on her neck.

She stood and grabbed the tray from Kiera. "So, what kind of appetizers did you make?" Jada asked in an attempt to steer the conversation away from "injuries" she didn't want to explain.

She followed Kiera out to her car to get the rest of the appetizers. When they returned, Mason was walking into the kitchen, buttoning the cuffs on a new, freshly pressed shirt.

"Hi," he said, giving Kiera a kiss on the cheek. "Did you win the bid for the Chamber of Commerce banquet?"

"I don't know yet. They still haven't contacted me."

"You need me to make a call?"

"No! I'd rather they choose me because they like my food, not because my big brother called in a favor, thank you very much."

"Fine," Mason said with a sigh. "I'm going out tonight so that I don't disturb your party." He glanced over at Jada. "Matthew Gauthier and I are going to talk about boring law stuff over dinner."

Jada didn't want to examine why her emotions went from mournful to euphoric in the span of two seconds. Though it wasn't as if she had to think very hard to figure it out. The thought of Mason going out with someone other than a colleague after the way he'd kissed her just minutes ago made her stomach hurt.

The fact that she had no right to feel any way whatsoever about who he went out with made her stomach hurt even more.

Jada cleared her throat. "There's a rumor going around that Matthew Gauthier is thinking of a possible state senate run," she said.

Mason hunched his shoulders. "Matt's being pretty tight-lipped about it, but if I were a betting man, I'd put my money on it that he will."

Matthew Gauthier was well-known and well-respected throughout Maplesville. His ancestors had founded the neighboring town of Gauthier.

"He would make a good senator," Jada remarked. "He's got the temperament for it."

Mason chuckled. "Yeah, I'm not sure how well I'd do in some of the situations Matt's found himself in."

Kiera held up both hands. "Hold on a minute. What's going on here? You two have been in each other's company for more than thirty seconds and you're not biting each other's heads off. That has to be a record."

That sexy half-smile formed on Mason's lips again. "Jada and I can be civilized to each other. Can't we, Jada?" He winked at her. "Have fun at the party," he said before turning for the door.

Jada tried not to stare as he made his way out of the house, but it was as if her brain had decided to rebel. She could not drag her eyes away. After Mason closed the door behind him, she turned to find Kiera staring her down with a probing, curious glint in her eyes.

"I guess we need to get back to work," Jada said. "We don't have much time before guests start arriving."

Kiera just continued to stare.

Jada pointed toward the dining room. "I'll...uh...I'll get back to it."

She got out of there before Kiera could ask any more questions.

***

Mason entered Emile's, located on Main Street in the heart of Gauthier, about twenty minutes from Maplesville. Not only was the food at Emile's some of the finest in south Louisiana, but it was the only restaurant within a thirty-mile radius that used cloth napkins. Everyone in Maplesville knew that if you were looking for anything more than casual dining, you had to make the drive to Gauthier.

There had been some bad blood between the neighboring towns in recent months. A growing number of Gauthier's residents felt that the new retail and eating establishments in Maplesville were encroaching on the family-owned businesses here in Gauthier. But if the crowded sidewalks he had to navigate through on his way to Emile's was any indication, Gauthier's residents had nothing to worry about. Main Street seemed more popular than ever.

As he made his way through the elegant dining room, Mason spotted Matthew Gauthier already seated at a table. As he approached, Matt stood, greeting him with a handshake and one-armed hug. The two of them had attended law school together. This area didn't boast many attorneys, so they tended to get together now and then to talk shop.

"Haven't heard from you in a couple of months," Matt said. "That big firm keeping you busy?"

"It's tax season," Mason answered, figuring it was answer enough.

Matt nodded, swirling the amber liquid around his highball glass before taking a sip. He tilted the glass toward Mason. "Want one?"

"No, thanks."

"Forgive me. I forgot only a thousand-dollars-a-bottle scotch touches those lips."

Mason shrugged off his friend's remark. "I don't drink much. When I do, I want it to be good."

The waiter came over to their table, and they both placed orders for Emile's famous crawfish etouffee. When the waiter left them, Matt folded his hands on the table and shot Mason a direct look. "Okay, what's going on? You said you needed to run something by me."

Mason let out a sigh, and for a minute,

reconsidered that drink. He gave Matt the condensed version of his dilemma over Oscar Davis's tax havens.

"The CPA sounds like a prick," Matt remarked.

"He's been the biggest pain in my ass," Mason said. "The thing is, I brought this client in expecting him to be my ticket to a partnership."

"But…?"

Mason glanced up at his friend, then brought his eyes back to the fleur de lis napkin ring he'd been fingering. "I'm not sure I can look past the gray areas, and it's driving me crazy," he admitted. "Remember when I vowed to be this cutthroat attorney back when we were in law school? What happened to *that* guy?"

"You were never that guy," Matt said. "Being cutthroat just isn't in you. And contrary to popular opinion, you and I both know that lawyers actually do possess souls."

Mason nodded. He looked over at his friend, his brow quirked in inquiry. "What about politicians?"

"Some of them do." Matt tipped his head back and emptied his highball. "And I haven't decided about the senate race, so don't ask."

Mason rolled his eyes. He knew Matt was holding out on him, but he had too much on his own plate right now to press him. If and when Matt called on him to help with a possible senate bid, he'd be there to offer assistance.

"Back to the reason you asked me to meet you for dinner," Matt continued. "I can tell this tax haven situation is weighing on your conscience."

"Of course, it is," Mason said. "I just keep thinking about how disappointed my dad would be if I sold out."

"You don't need to hear my opinion on this; you already have your answer."

"But I want that partnership," Mason said.

He just wasn't sure whether he was willing to pay such a high price. What good was a partnership if he wasn't able to look himself in the mirror?

When he woke the next morning, Mason moved on autopilot, getting dressed and doing what he had done nearly every Saturday morning for over a decade. He headed to his mother's for a pancake breakfast.

He entered the house and his mouth instantly watered at the aroma of spicy breakfast sausage.

"Good morning," Mason called as he walked into the bright yellow kitchen of the house his mother bought after their childhood home burned to the ground. His mom had been here longer than she'd been in their first house, but his father had never lived here, so for Mason, it never quite had the same feeling of home.

He walked over to his mother, who was at the stove nudging fluffy pancakes with her spatula, and gave her a kiss on the cheek.

"Hey, baby," she said, returning his kiss.

Kiera sat at the round breakfast table, clipping coupons from a stack of circulars. A few months ago, his mother had embarked on a coupon craze after seeing a show on television. Her garage was now packed with a bunch of stuff she didn't need, but that she insisted would one day come in handy.

"Why didn't you tell me you were leaving this morning?" Mason asked Kiera as he grabbed a mug from the cabinet and poured himself a cup of coffee. "We could have ridden over here together."

"I left your house since before six a.m.," she answered. "I've already put in two and a half hours at my kitchen this morning. I need to head back there in a little bit."

"Not until you've eaten breakfast," his mother said, carrying a platter piled high with pancakes and sausage to the table.

As they dug into their breakfast, their mother regaled them with the bargains she found at the outlet mall. She pointed at the circular Kiera held. "Cut out that coupon for two dollars off on diapers."

Mason rolled his eyes. "You do realize that if you're buying stuff you don't even need, it's not really saving you money, right?"

"I'm stocking up for when I finally have grandkids." She shot Mason a pointed look.

"Hey, why're you looking at me? You have a daughter right there who is more than capable of giving you grandkids."

"You're the oldest," Kiera said. "You're responsible for the grandchildren."

"I agree," his mother said.

"That's the most unfair thing I've heard today," he said. He gestured to Kiera. "FYI, that party you had last night won't help in the baby-making department." He looked over at his mother, his eyes creasing with mischief at the corners. "Do you want to know what kind of party your daughter had last night?"

"Oh, yes, the party! How did it go?" His mother asked. "I still need to put in my order."

Mason choked on the coffee he'd just sipped, and his mother and Kiera burst out laughing.

"Don't ever say that again," he warned.

"Mom's only teasing," Kiera said. "She put her order in since last week."

Mason dropped his fork and shoved his plate away. Who in the hell could still have an appetite after hearing that?

His mother and Kiera both laughed until they had tears rolling down their faces.

"I'd love to continue the torture," Kiera said, "But I need to get back to my kitchen."

She rose, kissed their mother's cheek, and carried her plate to the sink.

"Mason, the party I'm catering doesn't end until one a.m., which means I probably won't get in until close to three."

"Be safe, baby," her mother called.

Mason waited until he heard Kiera's car pull out of the driveway before he looked over at his mother and said, "Something's going on with her. She's been acting strange since she came to stay at my house."

"I think she's just stressed over everything happening with her condo. She also has some pretty big catering jobs coming up, and did she tell you that she may have a food booth at Jazz Fest? That's big time."

"It's more than that," Mason said. He hesitated a moment before he asked, "Has she mentioned anything to you about needing a loan?"

"A loan?" His mother's forehead furrowed. "Why would Kiera need a loan?"

He lifted his shoulders in a shrug. "That's what I want to know. A loan company called my house asking to speak to her. When I ask her what's going on she tells me that everything is fine, but it's obvious that something's up."

"You don't think she's in any kind of trouble, do you?"

Mason saw the brief flash of fear in his mother's eyes and his gut twisted. "It's probably nothing," he said, not wanting her to worry. "But just to make sure, I'm going to find out."

He started to rise, but his mother grabbed his arm. "Mason, don't go butting into your sister's business. You know what that will lead to."

Yes, he did. The last time he called himself helping Kiera, it did not end well. A rival catering company had put out false information about Catering by Kiera in an attempt to win a contract with a local film company. Mason had threatened to file a slander lawsuit, going so far as to have papers written up.

Kiera was furious. She accused him of treating her like a child and insisted he let her fight her own battles.

Since that incident Mason had done his best to maintain his distance when it came to Kiera's affairs, but dammit, he'd been stepping in to fight her battles ever since Buster Robinson tried to steal her snack money back when she was in the third grade. He was bound to slip up every now and then.

Something told Mason that whatever was happening with his sister right now was way worse than anything Buster had put her through.

He'd promised his dad that he would take care of both his mother and sister. It was a promise he'd kept for twenty years, and he wasn't about to go back on it now.

Kiera may not tell him what's going on, but he knew one person who likely knew the real story behind his sister's suspicious behavior.

The only question was, would he be able to

convince her to tell him?

Chapter Seven

Jada tilted her head back and let the warm spray wash over her. She grabbed the shampoo from the shower caddy and worked up a lather, groaning with pleasure as she massaged her scalp.

She'd stayed at Mason's until midnight helping Kiera clean up after the party. She refused to acknowledge that she had, at any time last night, stared toward his front door in hopes that he'd walk through it. In the same way she refused to acknowledge that she felt anything whatsoever when he hadn't made it back home by the time she left.

"Stop this," Jada warned herself.

Why should it matter to her whether or not Mason stayed out on a Friday night? Just because they'd shared two rock-her-world kisses, it didn't mean she had any say in what he did with his free time.

She blamed Eric for this. She had never been this insecure until she found out that bastard had cheated on her. Now she was feeling insecure about a man that wasn't even hers.

Jada rinsed out the shampoo. As she reached

for the conditioner, the stream of water coming from the shower turned from warm to ice cold. She yelped, jumping away from the spray. She got out of the shower and reached back in to turn the water off.

At least this time she was able to rinse out the shampoo. The last time this happened she had to finish rinsing out her hair in the kitchen sink. She pulled a bath towel from the shelf above the toilet, but before she could dry herself, furious pounding on her front door had her jumping out of her skin for the second time in less than two minutes.

Jada dropped the towel and grabbed her bathrobe from the hook. She pictured her neighbor on the other side of her front door, preparing to tell her that this dump of an apartment building was on fire.

She raced through her tiny living room and yanked open her front door, taking a step back when she discovered who was waiting on the other side.

"Mason," she said breathlessly. Whether it was due to her mad dash from the bathroom or just the sight of him, she didn't know. "What are you doing here?"

He just stared at her, his eyes traveling from her wet hair to her bare feet. Goose bumps instantly pebbled along her skin.

"I, uh, I came to ask you about Kiera," he said.

Jada's stomach bottomed out. "What about Kiera? Is something wrong?"

"That's what I want to know," Mason said, walking past her and into the apartment.

Jada closed the door and turned to him. He stood in the small space between her coffee table and TV stand, his arms crossed over his chest. His eyes re-embarked on that journey they'd taken just a moment ago, once again traveling the length of her body. His nostrils flared as he stared at her. He shucked out a weary breath and ran both palms down his face.

"God, you're naked under there, aren't you?" he said in a tortured voice.

Jada pulled the robe more securely around her neck. "I was getting out of the shower when I heard you knock," she said. "What is it you want to know about Kiera?"

"It can wait," he said, stalking toward her.

"Mason." She'd meant to say his name in a warning tone, but it came out more like a plea.

He stopped a hairsbreadth from her and brought his hand up to caress her cheek. The feel of his fingers on her bare skin sent a streak of desire shooting down her spine. How did he do that with just a simple touch?

Mason traced a finger along her jaw line. "Give me one good reason why I shouldn't kiss you right now," he murmured. "And don't say it's because we hate each other, because we both know that's not true."

Jada pushed out a ragged breath. "Damn. That's all I had."

A quick grin traced across his lips as he leaned over and connected them to hers. Jada released a soft whimper at that first contact. The minute his lips touched hers, she knew exactly what it meant for the rest of her day.

This time things were going much farther than just a kiss.

Mason shoved his hands in her hair, holding her head in place while his mouth plundered hers. In and out his tongue moved, invading her mouth, taking complete control of it.

Jada sensed when his left hand moved from her hair and traveled down her side. Then it moved to the front. He flattened his palm against her stomach before tugging on the sash at her waist. Seconds later, her robe fell open.

A moan climbed up her throat as Mason's palm snaked up her midriff to her breasts. He pinched and plucked and massaged her nipples, causing them to ache with a hunger Jada wasn't sure could be slaked. When had she *ever* felt a hunger like the one he was stirring within her?

"God, Mason," Jada groaned, her head falling back as his parted lips made their way up her neck.

She closed her eyes and focused on the incredible sensation of his warm, wet mouth against her skin. Each gentle bite, sexy tug, and indulgent lick set off a cataclysmic reaction within her. She felt his kiss all the way down to her toes. It made her belly quake and caused the spot between her legs to grow damp with want.

Their mouths never leaving each other, Mason shoved both hands inside her robe and clutched her ass, pulling her against him. He picked her up and Jada wrapped her legs around his waist as he carried her those few precious steps into her bedroom. For the first time, she was happy her apartment was so tiny. She couldn't survive a long trek to the bed.

Mason's lips traveled down her body as he laid her upon the bed.

"God, you're beautiful," he murmured against her stomach.

His thumbs swept back and forth over her nipples as he continued moving down her torso. Once he reached the aching spot between her legs, he wasted no time, using his fingers to spread her open and going straight for her clitoris. He sucked the throbbing nerves into his mouth, and Jada's back bowed off the bed, the motion pushing her further into Mason's face. He took full advantage, seizing her at the waist and holding her body still while his tongue lashed her with stroke after decadent stroke.

Her legs began to shake. Jada wasn't sure how much longer she could last before her entire being burst into flames.

It happened even quicker than she anticipated.

Mason drilled his tongue inside of her, and her body lit up, her release echoing throughout every corner of her body. She slowly opened her eyes to find Mason kneeling on the bed between her legs, yanking his shirt over his head. Jada made a feeble attempt to help him undress, but she was too weak to move.

He pushed his shorts and underwear down his hips, then grabbed his wallet and took out a condom. He ripped the package open and quickly rolled on the latex.

Jada pitched her head back and groaned toward the ceiling. "Oh, my God. I cannot believe we're doing this."

She felt Mason stiffen above her. She looked up at him.

"This isn't going to be one-sided, Jada. Do you want to do this or not?"

"I want it," she said, wrapping her arms around his neck. "I'll miss our legendary arguments, but I have a feeling you're about to make up for it."

Grinning, he said, "I'll figure out a way to occasionally piss you off if you want me to."

He scooped one arm underneath her hips and lifted her bottom off the bed as he entered her. Jada's entire being shivered with pleasure as he sank inch by gradual, delicious inch.

Gone was the serious lawyer. He obliterated every misconception she had as he took her body on the most sinfully erotic ride she'd ever had the pleasure of experiencing. Bracing himself above her with his hands on either side of her head, Mason slowly worshipped her body, gliding in and out with easy strokes, taking his time, trying different angles.

Jada squeezed her inner muscles, clutching his erection.

Mason gasped, his entire body stiffening.

"Do that again," he begged.

She obliged. With every forward thrust, she constricted her inner walls, clasping his thickness, holding it inside of her. Mason steadily increased his pace, his hips pistoning back and forth, propelling her to a place she wasn't sure she'd ever been before.

With one final thrust, Jada's entire world exploded. She locked her legs around Mason and held on while her body seemed to burst into a million pieces.

She had no sense of time passing as she lay in her bed, her limbs too weak to even conjure the thought of moving. She concentrated on pulling in deep breaths, the need to replenish her oxygen level on the same scale as when she exercised for a solid hour without stopping.

When Jada finally regained enough strength to open her eyes, she discovered Mason looking down at her, a sexy smile tilting up his lips.

"What?" she asked, covering her eyes with her forearm.

"You really are adorable."

She peeked at him. "I'm still not used to you calling me that."

"Okay, I'll stop."

"No!" she said quickly, drawing a laugh from him. Her lips hitched up in a lazy smile. "I said I'm not used to it. Not that I didn't like it."

"In that case," he said, lowering his head to her neck and giving her a gentle love bite. "I'll call you that from now on."

"Only when we're alone," she mandated.

He lifted his head. His brow peaked in quizzical inquiry, he asked, "What exactly does that mean?"

Jada covered her eyes again. "I don't know," she said. "It's stupid, but for some reason it feels as if being with you is some kind of offense against Kiera."

"That doesn't make any sense, Jada."

"Hence my use of the word 'stupid'." She let out a weary breath. "It's just that Kiera and I have been best friends for so long, and we tell each other everything. When I didn't tell her about what happened the night I ran out of gas, it was as if I faced a fork in the road and decided to take the path of deception."

"Are you always this deep after sex?"

"Shut up, Mason." She laughed.

He dipped his head low and captured her lips in another kiss before propping himself up on his elbow and resting his head on his balled fist.

"If you don't want Kiera to know that you're shagging her brother, that's fine with me. But if I have to keep this a secret, you'll need to make it worth my while."

Excited tremors fluttered around her stomach at the wickedly sexy glint in his eyes.

"What's going on in that head of yours?" Jada asked.

"Where do you keep that hot pink polka dot bag?"

The tremors in her stomach increased. So did Mason's grin.

"The front closet," she answered.

Placing a swift kiss on her lips, he pushed himself off the bed, and without a hint of modesty, walked his firm, naked ass out of her bedroom.

"Goodness," Jada whispered, covering her eyes again. "Who in the hell would have thought?"

***

Mason grabbed the innocent looking bag from the front closet's top shelf and carried it back to Jada's room. He found her sitting up in the bed, her naked body completely exposed.

How could she look so much better than she'd ever looked in his fantasies?

"Bring that here," she said, patting the bed.

His eyes widened. "A bit eager, aren't we?"

"Just earning your silence," she said.

He set the bag on the bed and Jada unzipped it.

"Hmm, where should we start?" Mason asked. "You're the expert here, I think you should decide."

The smile she sent his way was pure sin, and Mason got the distinct impression that this would go down in history as the best Saturday afternoon of his life.

"You know these are only supposed to be for selling purposes, right?" Jada asked. "If we use any of this, I'm going to have to buy another set to display when I do a party."

"I'll pay for everything in that damn bag," Mason said.

Her head flew back with her laugh. He tried to tear his eyes away from her breasts, but they were so perfect in every way imaginable, he just could *not* look away. But then Jada slipped a red, velvet bag from the travel case, and his eyes found something else to focus on.

The pouch had *The Masquerade Collection* embroidered across it in black script. Jada untied the drawstring, reached in, and pulled out several black sashes. She took one of the silken yards of material and stretched it across her breasts, dragging it back and forth across her nipples.

His knees damn near buckled.

"Do you trust me?" Jada asked.

Mason licked his lips and swallowed deep. "Depends on what you're planning to do."

"I promise I won't hurt you."

"I didn't say you couldn't hurt me."

She let out a playful, exaggeratedly shocked gasp. "Mason Coleman! Who in the hell knew?"

Mason climbed onto the bed. He twisted around and scooted back until his shoulder blades met the headboard. His breathing escalated as Jada pressed down on his shoulders, urging him to lie back on the mattress. She slipped a pillow underneath his head and tied the silken sash she'd been rubbing across her breasts over his eyes.

Mason swallowed a moan.

His pulse throbbed as she captured his right hand and tied another sash around his wrist. His arm was tugged upward as she tied the other end of the sash to the bedpost. She repeated it with his left hand.

Moments later, Mason flinched as he felt her soft lips upon his chest. The loss of his sight heightened the awareness of his sense of touch. He felt her on every inch of his skin.

She peppered him with delicate, silken kisses, trailing her tongue down the center of his chest, dragging the tip around his flat nipple before lightly flicking it across the distended nub. Mason hissed at her feather-light touch. He wanted more.

She kissed her way down his stomach, her

tongue swirling around his bellybutton before continuing its descent along the trail of hair that stretched from his navel to the erection that pulsed so hard it caused him physical pain.

"Jada," Mason moaned. He couldn't think of anything to say but her name. Coherent thought had left him the minute her lips had fallen upon his skin.

Her palm fisted around the base of his shaft and started a slow glide. She rubbed him up and down, increasing the pressure and speed.

When Mason felt the first wet sensation of her tongue on him, he nearly lost it then and there. He ground the back of his head into the pillow, clenching his jaw tightly as Jada's mouth covered his cock.

He reached for her, but was held back by the constraints imprisoning his wrists. He was dying to run his fingers through her hair, to clamp onto the back of her head and direct her movements as she sucked him long and hard. He wanted to tear the sash from his eyes so he could see her head bobbing up and down, to see his erection being swallowed into her hot, skillful mouth. Not being able to see her, not being able to touch her, it was pure, sweet torture.

Mason felt the intense throbbing that signaled an orgasm begin to build in his lower half. He clinched his fists, trying to hold off the inevitable.

Until Jada went all the way down, taking all

of him in her mouth, the tip of his cock hitting the back of her throat.

He lost it.

"Fuck!" Mason bit out, his hips bucking off the bed as he came in intense, hot spurts. And still she didn't relent, continuing to suck him until he'd released everything he had inside her.

He collapsed onto the bed, completely spent. The effort it took just to get air into his lungs was frightening. The woman damn near killed him.

"That's just the start," he heard Jada whisper against his ear. "But I think you'll need to lose the blindfold for what comes next."

Her hands went behind his head, releasing the sash. Her perfect breasts were just inches from his face, but before he could lunge forward to capture one with his mouth, she retreated. She reached back on the bed and brought another pillow forward, stuffing it underneath his head so that he sat up slightly.

Mason had no idea what she was preparing to do, but his heart began to pound in anticipation. She leaned over the edge of the bed where he'd placed the travel bag and came up with the blue dildo she'd wielded the other day.

"I seem to remember promising you a demonstration," she said, languidly looping the hard plastic around her breasts.

His stomach clenched as every muscle in his body tensed.

Her smile as naughty as anything he'd ever

seen before, she positioned herself between his legs, planting her feet on either side of his hips. Her knees slowly parted and she drew the tip of the dildo along her inner thighs, moving in unhurried circles.

Mason's breath came in hard pants as he watched her caress her skin with the toy. She swirled it up her stomach, to her breasts, teasing her nipples with the tip.

Jada levered herself up on one elbow, shooting him a devilish smile as she inserted the thick blue rod into her mouth. She sucked several times, coating it.

Mason knew what was coming next. His chest tightened as he waited for it.

As he'd anticipated, Jada pulled the wet dildo from her mouth and drove it inside of her, plunging the sex toy deep. Mason clamped his teeth down on his bottom lip to stop himself from crying out.

He looked on in excited, tortured fascination as Jada worked the dildo in and out, increasing the pace, her hips pumping with the motion, matching the thrust of her hands.

The soft cries rising from her throat fueled his desire. Mason pulled at the restraints. He needed to touch her so bad he could hardly breathe.

"Dammit, Jada. Untie me."

She didn't answer him. Her head was thrust back, her body writhing as she plunged the dildo inside of her with fast, furious strokes with one hand while the other circled her clit. Her legs began to tremble and her back bowed off the bed as she cried out.

Cum erupted from his cock, spurting over his stomach.

Mason collapsed on the bed again, trying hard to catch his breath. He wasn't sure if he even could, but if he died at this very moment, he would go with a smile on his face.

***

Jada sat cross-legged on a mountain of fluffy bedding, sucking peanut butter from a spoon. "I thought you said you needed to go to your office today," she said.

Mason looked up from where he was sprawled across the center of her bed. "Do you really think I would leave this? Be real, woman."

"Good," she said with a wink. "You shouldn't be working on a Saturday anyway."

"Now that I think about it, I can't remember the last time I took a Saturday off. I don't drive out to the firm, but as soon as I'm done with breakfast at Mom's, I'm in my home office all day and into the night."

"Mason, Mason, Mason. Always so responsible," she teased.

"I don't know any other way to be."

Jada sobered. After a moment, she spoke.

"You've shouldered a lot of responsibility for a very long time, haven't you?"

He shrugged. "I'm not complaining."

"You never do. For as long as I've known you, you've taken care of Kiera and your mother with very little complaint, and I know Kiera gave you a lot to complain about."

"Mainly because you were the one who would egg her on."

She grinned. "I was just trying to find ways to get under your skin. You were always so cool and calm. It was hard to get you riled up about anything."

"If you only knew... You didn't have to do anything to get me riled up, if you know what I mean." He wiggled his eyebrows and Jada doubled over with laughter. He dodged the pillow she threw at his head.

"I still don't believe you felt anything other than absolute disgust toward me back then. You just aren't that good of an actor, Mason Coleman."

"Are you kidding me?" He laughed.

Jada studied him as, still lying on his back, he grabbed the round throw pillow she'd pitched at him and tossed it up in the air.

"I used to especially love it when you would come over to the house after a basketball game without bothering to change out of your cheerleading uniform. You don't even want to know some of the things I imagined doing to you when I went into my room." He lolled his head to the side and grinned at her. "Actually, you made a couple of those fantasies come true a little while ago."

Jada threw her head back, her peal of laughter echoing off the ceiling. "Consider it an olive branch to make up for the things I got your sister into when we were in high school. I know we caused you a lot of headaches."

"You weren't too bad. If I was given the choice of which crowd I'd want Kiera to fall in with, it would have been you and Callie."

Jada put a hand to her chest. "My goodness. Who knew there was such a sweet guy living under all that starchiness?"

"Am I really that bad?"

"Yes," she answered without hesitation. "But I think I may have exacerbated your unflattering side. Kiera always said that you only turned into that serious, mean guy around me." She tilted her head to the side. "Why was that?"

He stared at her for a long time, still tossing the pillow up in the air. Finally, he set it aside and sat up in the bed.

"It's because I hated that you were with Eric. You could have chosen any other guy, and I would have at least been able to stomach it. But Eric Pearce?" He shook his head. "You were married to him for what, eleven years?"

"Twelve."

He grunted, shaking his head again. "I just don't know what you ever saw in him. He's always been such an asshole."

"Yes, but he was a charismatic one." A sad smile drew across her face. "I have to admit that I was blinded by the charm. Eric approached me the very first day I started at Maplesville High, and from that day forward I couldn't see anybody but him."

"I would look at the two of you walking around school, and I just wanted to rip his throat out. Eric never deserved you."

"I know that now, but it took me a while to see it." She swirled the spoon in the peanut butter, but found her appetite had suddenly fled. "It truly seemed as if I was living the fairytale every girl dreams about, until it all came crashing down. But the more I think about it, the more I realize that a part of me knew all along that Eric was being with other women. The signs were there for years, but I chose to ignore them because I didn't want to mess up the illusion of being the perfect couple."

"Were you happy?" Mason asked, scooting over to sit beside her and lifting the jar out of her hand.

"I thought I was," she said. "But, you know what? I am now. Even though I live in this little apartment—"

"Ridiculously tiny apartment," he interjected around a mouthful of peanut butter.

Jada stuck her tongue out at him. "Even though I'm living in this *cozy* apartment, and I'm barely scraping by some months, I'm more at peace now than I've been in a very long time."

"After putting up with Eric all that time, you deserve some peace." He trailed a finger down her cheek. "I'm happy you found the peace you were looking for."

Jada caught his hand. "What about you?"

"What about me?"

"Can you really be at peace with the way you shoulder everyone's problems, Mason? You spend so much time concerning yourself with what's going on with your mother and Kiera, I don't know how you have any time for yourself."

"Speaking of Kiera—"

"We're talking about you right now." She poked his chest. "You need to steal some time away to do something just for you."

"Hmmm…" He scooped up more peanut butter and sucked the spoon. "Let's see," he said after a few moments. "I've spent the majority of my day making love to you. That should definitely count as doing something just for me."

"Okay, I guess that does." She laughed.

"Now, back to Kiera."

Jada rolled her eyes. "Mason."

"Something is going on with her, Jada, and I know you know what it is."

"What makes you think that?"

"Because you, Callie and Kiera don't know how *not* to share everything that's going on in your lives."

"I haven't told her that I'm sleeping with her big brother."

"Because you only started sleeping with her big brother a few hours ago."

She rolled her eyes again. "Fine," she said with a sigh. "Kiera's in a tiny bit of a financial bind, but it's nothing she can't handle. Do *not* butt in, Mason. That's the last thing she wants, and I swear if you tell her I told you anything I'm going to deny it and then I'm going to run you over with my car."

"That's a sign of affection from you, isn't it?"

Jada reached over and pinched his nipple.

"Ouch, woman. Why are you so violent?"

"I mean it, Mason. Let Kiera handle this on her own. You've taken care of her long enough. She can fight this battle herself."

He remained silent.

"Mason," Jada said, warning coloring her voice.

"Fine." He sighed. "I'll stay out of it, even though it's ridiculous of her not to come to me for help when she knows all she has to do is ask. Why suffer through unnecessary trouble?"

"Because sometimes a person just has to do things for themselves. Deal with it."

This time he was the one to roll his eyes. Jada suddenly realized that as much as she'd enjoyed bickering with Mason over the years, it was a thousand times better when they bickered naked.

Mason reached over to her bedside table and picked up her alarm clock/iPod dock.

"Well, it doesn't make sense for me to try to get any work done today. And, since I've been forbidden to look into what's going on with my sister, I'll need something else to do with the rest of my Saturday."

Jada couldn't stop the naughty grin that etched across her lips. "What exactly did you have in mind?"

He leaned over the side of the bed and pulled the travel bag onto the mattress. "I think we can find a few things to occupy our time."

Chapter Eight

His legs crossed at the ankles atop his desk, Mason had just sat back in his office chair to look over a tax deduction app one of his colleagues had recommended for his clients, when the doorbell rang. Carrying the iPad with him, he continued scrolling as he made his way to the door.

He opened the door without even looking up. "Yeah?"

"Is that how you answer the door?"

His head shot up, along with his pulse rate.

"Hey there, beautiful," he answered with a smile, moving out of the way so that Jada could enter. He hadn't even realized how much he'd been waiting to see her until she appeared on his doorstep.

"You do realize that to hear you calling me beautiful is nearly as unsettling as you calling me adorable, right?"

"There's no denying you're beautiful," he said as he closed the door behind her. "And adorable still applies."

Her timid smile and gradually reddening cheeks only proved his point.

"Did Kiera decide to do that Seafood

Festival in Lafayette?" she asked.

Mason grinned at her change of subject.

"Yes, she did," he answered, setting the iPad on top of the nearby apothecary cabinet. He wrapped his arms around her and linked his hands at the small of her back. "Which means the house is empty. Which means that I'll be taking a break from work."

He went for her mouth, but she jerked her head back.

"Work? It's Sunday."

"It's also tax season, and I happen to be a tax attorney," he reminder her, aiming for her lips again. But Jada side-stepped him, ducking out of reach of his lips.

"I didn't come here for what you obviously have in mind," she said. "I came to kidnap you."

Mason arched a quizzical brow.

"You may want to put on some old clothes," she advised. "And tennis shoes, if you own a pair."

"I own tennis shoes."

"Then get them on."

"Can I know where we're going first?"

She scrunched her face up, as if she was thinking hard. "Hmm…do kidnappers usually tell their victims where they're going?"

"When the victim outweighs the kidnapper by sixty pounds? Yes."

"Fine," she exasperated. "We're going fishing. Yesterday you told me you haven't been since your dad died." She hunched her shoulders. "I was thinking that maybe it's one of those things you can start doing that's just for you."

Mason wasn't even sure what to do with the emotion that clogged his throat. The fact that she'd even given thought to coming up with something he could do that was just for him was more than any other woman he'd been with had ever done.

Last night, after making love for the fifth time in a twelve-hour span, Jada had cuddled against his back and asked him about the fire that would have likely killed him, his mother and his sister if he had not gotten up for a glass of water that faithful night. Recalling the fire eventually led to talk about his father, and he'd shared with her how much he used to love going fishing with him, and how he had not done so since his father passed away.

Mason knew he didn't have time to go fishing today. He was already behind after spending all day yesterday with her, though he'd cut his own tongue out before he voiced a single complaint about that. When he weighed the appeal of spending the day fishing with Jada — of doing *anything* with Jada — with being holed up in his home office all day reviewing spreadsheets, there really was no contest.

Twenty minutes later, they were heading east toward Gauthier.

"Where did you get the fishing equipment?" Mason asked, gesturing to the two rods sticking out the back window.

"I borrowed them from Bradley Mitchell," she said. "He owed me a favor after helping his daughter's dance team with their routine. See, those old cheerleader skills are still coming in handy."

"What about the uniform?" Mason asked. "I can think of several ways that can come in handy."

She plucked him on the arm. Damn, she was adorable.

She pulled off the highway onto a dirt road, and Mason suddenly realized where they were headed.

"Ponderosa Pond," he murmured. "Man, I haven't been here in years."

Memories of the last time he was here instantly bombarded him, but instead of making him melancholy, all he could do was smile. He tried his best not to think about those days just before he lost his dad, but after sharing those stories with Jada last night, he realized they were some of the best times of his life.

She parked underneath the overreaching branches of a huge oak tree, and they unloaded the rods and an aluminum pail from her car.

"What about bait?" Mason asked.

"Bait?"

"The fish won't just jump on the hook. We

actually need to cajole them into getting on there. The usual method is bait."

Jada let out a sigh. "Okay, if you want to know the truth, this is my very first time fishing, and I am so grossed out by the idea that it's taking everything I have within me not to throw up just thinking about it."

Mason chuckled, shaking his head. "Get in the car. We don't have to do this."

"No!" she said. "No, Mason. Really, I want you to fish."

He ran a finger down her cheek. "You're willing to be grossed out just for me? Do you realize how sexy that is?"

She laughed. "Do you realize how shocking it is to discover that you actually have a sense of humor?"

"I'm being totally serious," he said, swooping in for a quick kiss.

Using a sturdy branch, Mason dug around the softer earth at the edge of the pond and came up with a few worms. Jada freaked out so much when he baited his hook that Mason set her rod on the ground and declared that he would be the only one fishing. She responded by pumping a fist in the air.

"Now we just sit?" Jada asked.

"Pretty much."

She was silent for about a minute before she said, "So, is this right above watching paint dry on 'The Most Boring Things To Do in the World' list?"

Mason looked over at her. "You do remember that you're the one who brought me out here, right?"

"Yes," she said. "Are you enjoying it?"

"Actually, I am. It's been a really long time since I did this. I didn't think I ever wanted to fish again because I didn't think it would ever be the same without my dad. It might not be the same, but it's still good."

"According to Kiera, your dad was a laugh a minute."

"He was a huge practical joker. Used to drive my mom crazy."

"Yet, his son is so serious," she remarked. "Maybe you should take a page from your dad's book. He doesn't sound like a guy who would have been working on a Sunday."

"No," Mason said, a corner of his mouth turned up in a sad smile.

Over these past few weeks, thoughts about how his dad would view some of the decisions weighing on him lately had crossed Mason's mind more than once. He'd spent so much time concentrating on keeping that one promise he'd made to take care of Kiera and his mother that he never considered how his dad would feel about the way Mason was taking care of himself.

Something told him that the lighthearted family man who'd raised him would not approve. Jada had the right idea. There was nothing wrong with being a bit more selfish with his time. It wasn't as if he couldn't still watch over his mother and sister while also taking a little time out to enjoy life.

"Thank you for this," he said. "I didn't realize how much I needed it."

"You're welcome," she said, a surprised, genuine smile lighting up her face.

He switched his fishing rod to his left hand and reached for her, but she side-stepped him.

"Stay back," she said, crossing her fingers in an X to ward him off. "You're not touching me with those wormy fingers."

"You're such a girl." Mason laughed. "As long as I can touch you tonight, I have no problem keeping my wormy fingers to myself."

She grimaced. "You'll have to take a rain check. I have a bachelorette party coming up this week and still need to go through my inventory—"

"I can definitely help with that."

"I'd like to have some things available to sell at the bachelorette party, thank you very much." She laughed. "I also have to prepare for two interviews tomorrow, including one with The Fortier Foundation! They sent the email yesterday afternoon, but I was otherwise occupied."

Her grin was so deliciously sexy Mason had to stop himself from tossing the fishing rod in the pond and attacking those lips. But then her smile turned wistful, and the longing in her voice caused his chest to tighten.

"Mason, I want this job so badly. It would make all these months of searching worth it if my interview goes well tomorrow. Which is why I need to prepare."

The excitement he witnessed in her eyes had just earned Selena Pareja a bottle of her favorite Shiraz. Mason would have it delivered tomorrow. Even if Jada didn't get the job, it was worth it to see the pure happiness derived just from having an interview.

"In that case," he said, "I guess I'll have to be satisfied knowing that when I do cash that rain check, it's going to be worth my while."

She leaned forward, keeping the rest of her body at least a foot away from him, and touched her lips to his.

"If I get that job," she whispered seductively. "It will be off the charts."

Hmm...maybe he would send Selena a case of wine instead.

***

The effort it took to keep from smiling was harder than just about anything Jada had ever been through. There were times when she felt that things were possibly going in her favor, and there were times when she *knew* it.

She *knew* she was kicking ass in this

interview.

"I remember the chemical leak incident." Selena Pareja pointed to the addendum Jada had included with her résumé, outlining specific public relations issues she'd handled over the course of her career. "I'm pretty sure your spin on the situation saved the refinery a lot of money and headaches."

"The media was trying to make the spill out to be much more than it was. Not that I'm trying to excuse the refinery," Jada quickly added. The fact that her father was the plant manager at the time had stirred up enough of that type of rhetoric to last her a lifetime. "The entire incident could have been prevented if the workers had followed the standardized operating procedures, but as I explained in my many press conferences, the plant did everything they could to rectify the situation. I thought management handled it fairly."

"And *you* handled yourself remarkably well under the pressure," Selena said. "I don't envision you coming under that type of fire in this position, but people have questioned The Fortier Foundation's role in the community, and how our funds are allocated. We want someone who will be able to answer those questions without being intimidated."

"It takes a lot to intimidate me," Jada assured her.

"I can see that," Selena returned. She tossed

the addendum on her desk and folded her hands over it. "I have a couple of candidates that I've already promised interviews to, but based on this past hour, they will have to bring their A games if they want a chance at this position."

Jada's heart started to beat like a drummer in a rock band. The smile that drew across The Fortier Foundation's executive director's lips made it beat even faster.

Selena rose and offered her hand. Jada stood and captured it.

"Thank you so much for the opportunity to interview," she said, shaking Selena Pareja's hand.

"Believe me, the pleasure was all mine. I have a feeling you're going to save me a lot of time I didn't have to spare for interviewing."

Oh, my God! She was going to get this job!

"You'll be hearing from me soon," Selena said.

"I look forward to it," Jada answered. She picked up her purse from where she'd set it next to her chair, and turned to leave.

"Oh, and can you thank Mason for me, as well?" Selena called. "Tell him I owe him one."

Jada turned. "Excuse me?"

"Mason Coleman? He's the one who told me to keep an eye out for your résumé."

"I, uh, I didn't know," Jada said. "He never even mentioned that he knew you."

Selena shrugged. "We dated a while ago,

back when I was still practicing law. Mason's a sweetheart." She chuckled. "I'll be honest, when I agreed to interview you, I thought I was just doing him a favor, but it turns out he's the one who did me the favor. I'm happy he made that call."

Jada swallowed and forced a smile. "So am I," she said. "Thanks again."

As she made her way out of the downtown New Orleans office building, the anger flowing through her was so potent her hands shook with it. By the time she made it to the parking garage two blocks away, the tremors had subsided, but her jaw was still clenched with fury.

"Dammit!" Jada slammed her fists against her steering wheel.

For the first time ever, she thought she'd finally accomplished something based on her own merits. It wasn't because she was Montgomery Dangerfield's daughter, or Eric Pearce's wife. She wanted to land this job based on what she brought to the table, not because the man she was sleeping with called in a favor to his ex-girlfriend!

"Dammit, Mason!"

She started the engine and threw the car into reverse, and had to slam on her breaks when she nearly backed out into an oncoming car.

"Okay, you need to calm the hell down," Jada said, gripping the steering wheel. She took several deep breaths before easing out of the parking space and exiting the garage.

She waited until she was out of city traffic and on the expressway heading back to Maplesville before she fished her cell phone from her purse and dialed Kiera. She didn't even waste time with a greeting.

"You will not believe what your brother did," Jada opened.

"The same way I don't believe what *you* did," Kiera bit out.

Jada jerked with a start at the bitterness in her friend's voice. "What did I do?"

"You told Mason about me losing that money with the food truck."

Jada's one-handed grip tightened on the steering wheel.

Damn you, Mason!

"Kiera, I did not tell him any specifics."

"You shouldn't have told him anything at all!" Kiera screeched.

"He asked me what was going on with you the other night, and all I said was that you were in a bit of a bind. And I specifically told him to stay out of it."

"He didn't listen," Kiera said. "And just when in the hell did you start screwing my brother? Is this some kind of game the two of you have been playing behind everyone's back, pretending you hate each other when people are around, yet sneaking around to sleep with each other? If I had known my financial troubles would become the subject of yours and Mason's pillow talk, I wouldn't have said anything in front of you."

"Kiera, please," Jada pleaded. "You know you can trust me with anything."

"That used to be the case. It's not anymore," she said before hanging up.

Jada briefly shut her eyes, trying to blot out the rage she'd heard in her friend's voice. She knew how much it meant to Kiera to handle this problem on her own. Just as much as it had meant to *her* to get the job at The Fortier Foundation on *her* own.

Jada started to dial Mason's number, but then she tossed the cell phone on the passenger seat. If ever there was a conversation that needed to be handled face-to-face, this was it.

Chapter Nine

Mason raised two fingers in a casual wave to the security guard before driving through his subdivision's wrought-iron gate. It had never felt so good to be so close to home. He could taste the scotch he so desperately needed after his rough day, despite leaving the office early.

Giving up Oscar Davis's account was probably both the hardest and easiest thing he'd ever done in his career. The partnership that had seemed so close slipped a bit farther out of his reach, but the weight that had lifted off his shoulders the minute he officially handed the account to his colleague, Charles Boudoin, made up for it. Let Charles deal with Davis and his bulldog CPA.

Most importantly, Mason felt as if he could now look himself in the mirror without questioning the integrity of the man staring back at him. He didn't have to wonder whether or not his dad would be proud of his decision. Mason *knew* he would be.

He turned into his driveway and pressed the garage door opener. As he waited for the door to rise, he sent Kiera another text message, explaining why he'd transferred the money she refused to accept into her bank account. It shouldn't be this damn hard to give somebody ten thousand dollars. He only hoped it was enough to cover whatever she had considered borrowing from that loan company in Hammond.

Just as he pulled into the garage, a white car turned into the driveway.

A smile drew across his face. He'd been thinking about that rain check Jada had promised all day.

He got out of his car at the same time Jada exited hers. He started toward her, but his steps slowed as he took in the look on her face.

They met up just outside of the garage.

"What in the hell is wrong with you?" Jada asked. "Seriously, Mason, is it just impossible for you to stay out of other people's business?"

"What are you talking about?"

"Where should I start? Maybe with you begging your freaking ex-girlfriend to give me a job? Or how about butting your nose in your sister's financial problems when I told you specifically to stay the hell out of it," she screamed.

"You want to calm down?" Mason asked, trying his hardest to remain calm himself.

"Do I look like I want to calm down?" she yelled.

He put both hands up. "I'm not doing this in my front yard."

He turned and walked to the front door. Instead of slamming it like he wanted to do, he held it open. He knew Jada would follow.

She didn't disappoint.

She stomped into the house and Mason closed the door behind her.

Stopping just inside the entryway, she turned and threw her hands up in the air. "Why, Mason?"

"Why what?" he threw back at her. "Why did I call a contact with the company that you have your heart set on working for and put in a good word for you? I don't know, I guess I just felt like being a bastard."

"She's not just a contact, Mason. She was your girlfriend."

"Selena and I broke up years ago."

Her palms flew in the air. "You know what? I don't even care. What she was to you personally doesn't even matter. It's the fact that you stuck your nose in where it didn't belong. I did not want your help, Mason. I wanted to get this job on my own. How am I supposed to know whether or not they really want *me*?"

"Selena Pareja isn't going to give you a job if she doesn't want to. We weren't that damn close."

She covered her face with her hands. "God, Mason. You just shouldn't have done it. And what about Kiera?"

"What *about* Kiera? She was in trouble, and

it's my job to help her when she's in trouble."

He started to pace, because what in the hell else could he do to release this pent up frustration?

"When are you going to accept the fact that your sister does not need you stepping in to be her knight in shining armor all the time? Let her do things for herself like the adult she is."

"Look, Jada, I don't care what you say. I was not going to sit around and let her pay a bunch of interest on a loan when I had the money in the bank. If Kiera needs something, she should come to me. She knows I'm here for her."

"Yes, she does. So the fact that she didn't come to you should tell you something. Kiera would have found a way to make the money. I would have helped her if necessary."

Mason stopped in front of her.

"How? By bringing her into your little consulting business? Forgive me if I don't want my baby sister selling fluorescent-colored cocks for a living."

She took a visible step back, her mouth agape. With venom in her eyes, she said, "Kiss my ass, Mason." Then she turned and stormed out the house, slamming the door behind her.

Mason pitched his head back and rubbed between his eyes.

"Shit," he whispered.

He blew out a weary breath and walked back to the garage, taking his briefcase from his trunk, and lowering the garage door. Then he went into his office, tossed the briefcase on the desk, and headed straight for the scotch.

Mason poured himself a finger and downed it in one gulp, then he filled the short tumbler a third of the way and carried it to his desk, plopping down in the chair and resting his head against the soft, leather headrest.

That sure as hell wasn't what he'd expected when he spotted Jada's car driving up.

What was it with the women in his life? Forget about being grateful for the help he offered; both Jada and Kiera had gone crazy as hell over it.

"I was just trying to help," Mason blew out. He sipped his scotch and set the glass on the desk. Then he ran his palms down his face.

Maybe he should have listened when Kiera, *and* Jada, *and* his mother told him to stay out of it. Maybe he should have just let Kiera handle this on her own, even though it made no damn sense whatsoever for her *not* to get the money she needed from him. She knew he was always here for her.

But what would happen if he wasn't?

Mason bolted upright in the chair. He braced his elbows on the desk and rested his lips on his folded hands, contemplating a scenario he had never bothered to consider.

He knew first-hand just how quickly someone you thought would always be there could leave your world in an instant.

His eyes pinched closed against the memories that refused to be suppressed. He remembered the conversation like it happened twenty minutes ago instead of twenty years. Remembered the pride on his father's face, and how he'd praised Mason for stepping in when his family needed him. Remembered how his dad told him that he felt relieved knowing that Mason would be there, even if he wasn't around.

Mason's throat tightened as he recalled how his dad had laughed when Mason covered his ears and told him that he didn't want to talk about what would happened if he died. His dad had assured him that he would be around for a long time; he was only telling him those things as a precaution. The house fire had showed them all that anything could happen.

And the following day, it had.

At fourteen-years-old, Mason had never imagined he would be required to step up to the plate so soon. What would have happened if his dad had not prepared him for life without him? Would he have been able to take care of his mother and Kiera the way he had all these years?

Anything could happen to him: car accident, heart attack like his father, a building collapsing on top of him. There was no guarantee that he would be here. If he didn't start allowing Kiera to handle her own problems, things would only be harder for her if the unpredictable came to pass.

As for Jada…

Mason tossed the rest of the scotch down his throat, then shot up from his chair. He paced in front of his desk, recalling the look on her face when she'd stormed out of the house.

It hadn't taken him long to recognize that calling Selena on her behalf was a tactical mistake of epic proportion. All he had to do was imagine how he would feel if she called in a favor to Eric for him. Just picturing the hypothetical made his jaw clench.

Mason stopped in front of the window, staring at the buds forming on the silver maples lining the backyard.

He prided himself on his ability to methodically think his way through any problem, but he had no idea how he was going to fix this one.

***

Jada raised her head when she heard the roar of a car engine, but she remained seated in the spot she'd occupied on Callie's porch for the past hour. Her friend climbed out of her SUV, still wearing her lab coat.

"I'm sorry I couldn't come right away," Callie said. "I got behind with patients this morning and found myself playing catch-up all day."

"It's okay," Jada said, waving her off with one hand as she wiped a wayward tear with the other.

Callie sat next to her on the second to the last porch step and covered Jada's knee. "What in the heck happened between you and Kiera?"

Jada took a moment to collect herself before giving Callie the abbreviated version of what had transpired over the past couple of weeks, starting with the night she'd run out of gas on her way home from the Naughty Nights party. When she admitted that she and Mason had started sleeping together, Callie sprung up from the porch step like it was on fire.

"You and Mason? Mason Coleman? The same Mason Coleman you said you would drench in honey and pitch into a pile of red ants if it wasn't for the fact that he was Kiera's brother?"

"Yes," Jada droned. She lifted her palms up in bewilderment. "I'm not even sure how it happened. We both...I don't know...misunderstood each other all these years. Anyway, when we were together the other day he asked me if I knew what was going on with Kiera."

"You didn't." Callie groaned.

"I just told him that she was in a bind. I didn't mention the food truck or anything to do with her catering company. He must have figured that out on his own, and of course, he stuck his nose into her business." Jada let out a sigh. "Now Kiera hates me."

She didn't even mention what Mason had done to *her*. It was too demoralizing to even think about it. Besides, the job with The Fortier Foundation meant nothing when compared to her friendship with Kiera.

Callie pulled out her cell phone. "I know we still have a few weeks before our normal monthly wine and whine session, but these are special circumstances."

"She won't come over if she knows I'm here," Jada said. Hurt radiated in her chest at the admission.

"She can't avoid you forever, so why do it at all?" Callie reasoned.

Stuffing her free hand in the pocket of her lab coat, she walked along the brick-laid walkway that led up to her house. Even though she spoke in low tones that made it impossible for Jada to make out what she was saying, the expression on her face said it all. After a couple of minutes, Callie walked back over to the porch and reclaimed her seat on the step.

"She'll be here in ten minutes," she announced.

Jada whipped her head toward her. "Really? How did you do that? She wouldn't even talk to me."

"She doesn't know you're here," Callie said.

Jada closed her eyes and covered her face in her hands. She felt Callie's arm come around her shoulders and nearly sobbed with gratitude at the support her friend provided. They remained there, sitting quietly. One offering comfort, the other gratefully accepting it.

Nearly twenty minutes went by before Kiera's SUV pulled in behind Callie's.

Jada sprung up from the step. She stood and watched as Kiera climbed from behind the wheel, shut the door, and locked it with her key fob. The resentment furrowing her brow caused a heavy weight to settle in Jada's stomach, but the fact that she had not backed out of the driveway the minute she saw her sitting on the porch step was a positive sign.

Jada rubbed her palms down the sides of her pants as she prepared to beg and plead for her friend's forgiveness.

Kiera walked up to them, and folded her arms over her chest.

"Well," Callie said, slapping her palms on her thighs and pushing herself up. "I'll go and get the wine."

"It's four in the afternoon," Kiera said.

"What the hell does that have to do with anything?" Callie asked as she went into the house.

Kiera rolled her eyes, then brought them back to Jada.

"I'm sorry," Jada opened.

"I know," Kiera said.

When she saw the small smile creep along the edges of her friend's mouth, Jada's heart blossomed with hope. She closed the distance between them and smothered Kiera in a hug. When she realized Kiera was holding on just as tight, a small cry of relief broke past her lips.

"I'm sorry for the things I said to you," Kiera said. She pulled away slightly, but still held onto Jada's arms. "And I'm actually ecstatic that you're screwing my brother."

Jada choked out a laugh. "I could cheerfully murder him if I saw him right now," she said.

"No, no. Don't." Kiera shook her head. "Let me do that, after I stuff the ten thousand dollars he keeps transferring to my bank account down his throat."

Callie came outside with three plastic cups stacked together in one hand and a bottle of Riesling in the other. "Couldn't handle wine glasses," she said, holding up the stack of cups. She looked back and forth between Jada and Kiera. "Are we good?"

"We're good," Kiera said.

"Yes," Jada answered at the same time.

"Good." Callie nodded. "Now why don't we sit out here so Jada can tell us how she ended up in bed with her biggest enemy? Well, biggest enemy after Eric, of course."

"The bastard," the three of them said in unison.

Jada and Kiera both sat on the wooden swing on Callie's huge wraparound porch, while Callie perched her hip on the railing, her back against the thick post. As they sipped white wine from plastic cups, Jada gave them the extended version of her whirlwind courtship with Mason, halting whenever Kiera told her that it was getting into things-a-baby-sister-doesn't-need-to-know-about-her-brother territory.

Jada struggled to maintain her calm as she told them about the interview with The Fortier Foundation and the mini bombshell Selena Pareja dropped in her lap as she was leaving the office.

"My God! How can someone so damn smart be so damn clueless?" Kiera screeched.

"Ask him yourself," Callie said. She nudged her chin forward, and both Jada and Kiera twisted around on the porch swing. Mason was walking toward them. He'd parked his car in front of Callie's neighbor's house.

Jada's stomach clenched with yearning at the sight of him, even while her hands balled into fists. With every inch closer he came, her heart beat faster and faster, to the point that she could hardly hear anything past the blood rushing in her head by the time he made it to the house.

He stopped a few feet shy of the landscaping that lined the base of the porch, both hands shoved in his pants pockets.

"Hi," Mason said.

Callie was the only one who responded with actual words.

"Hi, Mason," she said.

Kiera grunted. Jada remained silent. Speaking past the emotion in her throat was beyond her capabilities at the moment.

His warm brown eyes were shadowed with pain, his internal turmoil blatantly obvious.

"Jada," he opened. The word came out hoarse. He winced, swallowed, released a quick, anguished breath, and tried again. "Jada, can I speak to you? Privately?"

For a moment she debated whether or not she would ever speak to him again, but she knew that was just her anger talking. She recalled Callie's earlier words. She couldn't avoid him forever, so why do so at all?

Jada pushed herself up from the swing. The relief that flashed across Mason's face nearly caused her to race down the porch steps and wrap her arms around him, but she thankfully nipped that impulse just in time. At least make the man work for her forgiveness.

He met up with her at the newel post at the bottom of the steps. "Walk with me?" he asked.

She gave a slight nod, and they started up the walkway. Mason turned back. "I'll talk to you tonight, Kiera."

She replied with another grunt.

———

They continued up Callie's walkway and onto the sidewalk, strolling at an easy pace past his car, neither saying anything. Jada breathed in a lungful of the sweet, white jasmine-scented air while she tried to process everything that had happened today. It already felt like the longest day ever, and she knew the conversation looming ahead of them would only add to the day's endless feeling.

They reached a small park with several pieces of playground equipment. Despite the dearth of verbal communication between them, their feet led them both to the empty swing set. Jada positioned herself on the concave rubber seat and wrapped each hand around a metal chain. She toed the ground, lightly rocking her swing back and forth.

"Saying I'm sorry doesn't even begin to cover it," Mason started. "But I need to say the words, so…I'm sorry."

Jada bit her bottom lip. After several moments passed, she looked up at him, and asked, "For which part?"

"All of it," he said, his voice cracking on the words. He shut his eyes briefly, slipped one hand out of his pocket and massaged the back of his neck. "I've spent more than half my life taking care of the women in my life, Jada. Making sure my mom and Kiera never have to worry about anything is as natural as breathing for me. It's what I do."

"I know that," she said.

"I saw how much you wanted that job, and when I found out it was with Selena's company I realized that I could help, and that's the only thing that mattered." He shook his head and choked out a humorless laugh. "Now that I think about it, I realize how ridiculous it was.

"Don't let my stupidity stop you from taking this job, Jada. Selena left me a message on my phone—" His hands shot up. " —it was all about you. She loved you. She thinks you're perfect for this job and the entire message was her singing your praises and thanking me for clueing her into you as a candidate."

"It was a great interview," she mumbled. She looked straight ahead, staring at the budding leaves on the maples as they fluttered in the soft breeze. "Before I found out that the two of you were bed buddies, I actually liked Selena."

"Jada, don't….shit," Mason whispered.

She looked up at him and decided to put him out of his misery. "I'm going to accept the job if she offers it, Mason."

His eyes widened. "She's going to offer it," he said. "I have no doubt that she will."

Jada hoisted herself out of the swing and closed the distance between them. She captured Mason's hands, entwined their fingers, and gently swung their arms back and forth.

"Calling Selena wasn't the smartest move

you've ever made, but it was probably one of the sweetest. You weren't trying to control me, you were just trying to help."

"That's all," he said.

"Judging by what I saw of her personality, I know Selena would not offer me a job if she didn't think it was best for The Fortier Foundation, and that makes a huge difference. *If* I am offered the job, it will be because she believes I'm the best person for it."

"There's no *if* about it."

She hunched her shoulders. "I won't let myself get excited until after I receive an official offer."

They stood there for several quiet moments, holding hands.

Mason finally broke the silence. "Please tell me I haven't messed this up. I've spent much of my adult life trying to avoid the feelings I have for you, but now that I've put it out there, I don't want to take it back. I can't.

"*Please*, tell me you won't end this because of what I did. We're just starting, Jada."

The naked pain in his voice wrapped itself around her soul.

Jada pulled her trembling bottom lip between her teeth and shook her head. "I don't want it to end," she whispered.

His face crumbled in relief as he pulled her against him, wrapping his arms around her. His hands came up to capture her face as his mouth lowered onto hers.

"Thank you," he murmured against her lips. "Thank you, thank you, *thank you*."

Jada melted against him, clasping her hands behind his head and thrusting her tongue into his mouth. The heady sensation of his heat and strength and flavor spiraled through her veins, erupting in an exquisite burst of pleasure that reverberated throughout her bloodstream.

Mason gradually pulled his lips away and rested his forehead on hers. Their breaths mingled as they both panted, trying to recover from the kiss that she still felt in every part of her body.

"I can't promise you that I won't mess up again," he said in a hushed voice. "Like I said, I've been doing the caretaker thing most of my life. It may take me a while to turn it off."

"I won't hold it against you if you slip up every now and then. Kiera, on the other hand, may commit bodily harm."

Mason winced. "I'm not looking forward to facing her."

"She's been putting up with you sticking your nose in her business for thirty-two years, Mason. She'll forgive you. She won't take your money, but she'll forgive you."

His brow quirked. "You sure about that?"

"Positive. Just give her some time." She brought her arms around his waist and linked her hands at the small of his back. "In the meantime, I think we should do this for a little while longer."

Then she lifted her face to his and captured his lips.

Epilogue

Mason carried the army green tackle box he'd found in the garage at his mother's house, depositing it on his kitchen table. After finishing his pancake breakfast, he, his mother and Kiera had gone on an expedition, searching every corner of the garage for the tackle box his father used to keep behind the seat of his pickup. It was one of the few things of his that had not perished in the fire with everything else they'd owned.

Mason had to use a butter knife to pry the rusty clasp lock apart. Once inside, he wasn't surprised to discover that the twenty-year-old hooks, jigs, and sinkers were as old and tarnished as the lock, but that didn't matter. He'd spent hours at the outdoorsman shop, buying all-new tackle gear and a top-of-the-line graphite rod and reel. The tackle box is what he wanted. That was the important thing.

It had been a month since Jada had taken him fishing, and every weekend since his skin had tingled with the urge to get out there and cast a line. When he left his office yesterday, he made a decision. He would take at least one weekend a month for himself. Whether he went fishing, took a drive out to the Gulf Coast, or just hung around the house watching marathons of *Law & Order SVU*, it would be his time to do whatever he felt like doing.

Mason emptied the rusty tackle into the trash and soaked a dish towel so he could wipe out the inside of the tackle box. Just as he was finishing up, the doorbell rang. He tossed the towel on the table, wiped his hands on the front of his faded T-shirt, and jogged to the door.

He spotted Jada through the front door's beveled glass. Mason opened it and leaned against the door jamb.

"Morning, beautiful," he greeted. His eyes crinkled as he gestured toward the raincoat she was wearing. He looked up at the sky. It was a brilliant blue without even the hint of a cloud. "You know something I don't know about the weather today?"

"No," she said, stepping inside the house. She turned and slipped the raincoat off her shoulders. "I was just hoping you were in the mood for something a little bit naughty."

Mason's gut instantly tightened. "Where did you get that?"

"Some things are too special to part with." She struck a pose in her tiny maroon and gold Maplesville Mustang Cheerleader uniform. "What can I say? I'm sentimental."

"Sexy as hell is what you are," Mason said,

his voice rough with the lust rapidly invading every single fiber of his body.

"Does that mean you *are* feeling a little bit naughty?" she asked. "Because I have my hot pink polka dot case in the car. We can come up with a bunch of fun things to do to pass the time."

Mason sauntered toward her and hooked a finger in the V-shaped collar of the snug-fitting uniform, and pulled her to him. "There's nothing little about the kind of naughty I'm feeling."

"Good," Jada whispered against his lips. "Because I'm about to give you all the naughty you can handle."

— The End —

Thank you so much for purchasing and reading *A Little Bit Naughty*.

If you haven't done so yet, be sure to read Callie and Stefan's love story in the first novella of the *Moments in Maplesville* series, **A Perfect Holiday Fling**!

If you enjoyed this story, please consider checking out my other romances, including my Bayou Dreams series, set in the fictional town of Gauthier, Louisiana.

***

The Holmes Brother Series:

Set in New Orleans, the Holmes Brothers series follows the lives of Elijah, Tobias, and Alexander Holmes as they find love in one of the world's most romantic cities.

Read **Deliver Me**, **Release Me**, and **Rescue Me**, available both individually and in a special bundle edition!
Get all three books in the Holmes Brothers series for one low price!

***

In Her Wildest Dreams
Event planner Erica Cole recruits her best friend to help her plan the ultimate Valentine's Day fantasy, but chocolatier Gavin Foster is determined to show her that they should be more than just friends.

***

The Rebound Guy
Relationship advisor Dexter Bryant is trying to shake his stud-for-hire image, but when Asia Carpenter makes him an offer he can't refuse, Dex will have to play the role of professional rebound guy one last time.

Romances from Harlequin Kimani!

The New York Sabers
*Don't miss my sizzling **New York Sabers** football*

---

series! Check my website for details!

Bayou Dreams
Check out my brand new series set in the small, fictional town of Gauthier, Louisiana!

About the Author:

A native of south Louisiana, Farrah Rochon officially began her writing career while waiting in between classes in the student lounge at Xavier University of Louisiana. After earning her Bachelors of Science degree and a Masters of Arts from Southeastern Louisiana University, Farrah decided to pursue her lifelong dream of becoming a published novelist. She was named *Shades of Romance Magazine*'s Best New Author of 2007. Her debut novel garnered rave reviews, earning Farrah several SORMAG Readers' Choice Awards. *I'll Catch You*, the second book in her New York Sabers series for Harlequin Kimani, was a 2012 RITA[R] Award finalist.

When she is not writing in her favorite coffee shop, Farrah spends most of her time reading her favorite romance novels or seeing as many Broadway shows as possible. An admitted sports fanatic, Farrah feeds her addiction to football by watching New Orleans Saints games on Sunday afternoons.